"Pleased to meet you, Ms. Gould."

It appeared Logan was happy to pretend he'd never met Honor before. Never met her, never kissed her, never touched her body so intimately that Honor was in danger of flaring into a plume of smoke at the sheer memory of what Logan had done to her, with her. But she could see the questions in his eyes and she knew she'd have to face them down.

She hadn't anticipated the electricity that sizzled through her palm as his larger hand firmly clasped hers.

"And you, too, Mr. Parker," she finally managed to say. "Your arrival here is quite a surprise."

"I can imagine," Logan Parker replied.

Was that a twinkle in his eye? Did he find this situation funny? She had to clarify this situation and ensure that he would keep what they'd done strictly between them.

But could she trust him?

* * *

Seducing the Lost Heir by Yvonne Lindsay
is part of the Clashing Birthrights series.

Dear Reader,

Welcome to the first in my new series, Clashing Birthrights! Like many people, I'm often drawn to news stories about babies being swapped at birth (by accident or design), or stolen at birth and as adults finding their true families. These situations always get me thinking.

For this book, *Seducing the Lost Heir*, Logan Parker discovered on his "mother's" death that she wasn't his birth mother after all! In fact, she'd stolen him from the nursery after her own baby had died and spirited Logan away. Feeling as though his whole life has been a lie, he's determined to claim the life and family, including his identical twin brother, he's never known.

Poor and disadvantaged all her childhood, Honor Gould is determined to climb the corporate ladder at Richmond Developments any way she can. Even if it means marrying the boss's son and heir apparent, Keaton Richmond. When her fiancé surprises her one night at a conference hotel, the last thing she expects to discover the next morning is that she's slept with the wrong twin!

Thank you for picking up *Seducing the Lost Heir*. I hope you will enjoy reading Logan and Honor's journey to a true happy-ever-after and that you will keep an eye out for Keaton's story, *Scandalizing the CEO*, coming soon!

Happy reading!

Yvonne Lindsay

YVONNE LINDSAY

SEDUCING THE LOST HEIR

HARLEQUIN

DESIRE

HARLEQUIN®
DESIRE™

ISBN-13: 978-1-335-20953-5

Seducing the Lost Heir

PLEASE RECYCLE
THIS PRODUCT IS RECYCLABLE

Recycling programs
for this product may
not exist in your area.

Harlequin Enterprises ULC
22 Adelaide St. West, 40th Floor
Toronto, Ontario M5H 4E3, Canada
www.Harlequin.com

Printed in U.S.A.

Award-winning *USA TODAY* bestselling author **Yvonne Lindsay** has always preferred the stories in her head to the real world. Married to her blind-date sweetheart and with two adult children, she spends her days crafting the stories of her heart. In her spare time she can be found with her nose firmly in someone else's book.

Books by Yvonne Lindsay

Harlequin Desire

Wed at Any Price

Honor-Bound Groom
Stand-In Bride's Seduction
For the Sake of the Secret Child

Marriage at First Sight

Tangled Vows
Inconveniently Wed
Vengeful Vows

Clashing Birthrights

Seducing the Lost Heir

Visit her Author Profile page at Harlequin.com, or yvonnelindsay.com, for more titles.

You can find Yvonne Lindsay on Facebook, along with other Harlequin Desire authors, at Facebook.com/harlequindesireauthors!

This book is dedicated to all the amazing people (including some of my own family) who had to stay on the front lines and put themselves at risk during the pandemic. I salute and thank you all!

One

She'd only had two glasses of champagne, but she was already beginning to feel a little buzzed. Definitely time to stop drinking alcohol. Honor Gould had learned the hard way, by watching her mom, what happened when buzzed turned to drunk and drunk turned to dangerous and stupid decisions.

The noise in the downtown Seattle hotel bar had reached deafening levels as conference delegates poured in. It never failed to amaze her to see so many people who could be totally professional in their day-to-day business get so messy when they let their hair down. She rarely let go of her rigid self-control, and certainly never among strangers. No, Honor had a plan, and getting a little too drunk or a little too loud was not anywhere on her list of things to do.

One of her fellow conference delegates passed her a fresh glass of champagne. Honor shook her head.

"No, thanks, I've had enough," she said firmly.

"Aw, come on. It's not every year you get to celebrate being commercial interior designer of the year," the guy protested, pushing the flute of sparkling golden liquid back in her direction.

To shut him up, Honor accepted the glass and lifted it in a toast, but the glass never made it to her lips.

"Thank you," she said with a smile that masked her irritation.

"That's more like it," he said. Then, to her relief, he turned his attention to a new group of people coming into the bar, their raucous laughter filling the air.

Honor moved away from the crowd to find a quieter spot at the end of the bar. From here she could do her usual observations before heading up to the room she'd booked to ensure she'd be fresh for the early session she was presenting tomorrow morning before going into work. She doubted the session would be particularly well attended, given that many of her fellow conference goers would likely need to sleep in after tonight. But that didn't bother her. She was mostly interested in adding the presentation to her résumé. After dragging herself up from the gutters her mother had been satisfied dwelling in, Honor was on a trajectory to success and wealth of the kind she'd perpetually dreamed as a little girl. The award at the dinner tonight, her presentation at this prestigious conference—they were all tiny steps along the way to reaching her goals. To security. Comfort. Choices.

She put the untouched champagne flute on the bar behind her and ordered a sparkling mineral water from one of the bar staff, who were run off their feet with the steady influx of patrons. She'd drink her water and head back up to her room. No one would notice she was missing, and it would give her an opportunity to go over her notes for tomorrow again.

Honor had just received her drink and raised the glass to her lips for a sip when she felt a frisson of awareness send a trickle of heat down her spine. She turned slightly, her gaze instantly arrested by the arrival of a newcomer to the bar.

Keaton? He was here? Had he come to surprise her?

She couldn't believe her eyes. Her fiancé was not a man of spontaneous actions. When she'd told him she'd be at the hotel for the conference for two days, he'd merely nodded and continued with his work. When she'd invited him to attend the awards dinner as her plus-one, he'd mentioned some business dinner he couldn't get out of. And yet, here he was, heading past the bar toward a small table set against a wall.

He was a handsome man. A real head-turner. But Keaton always acted as if he was completely unaware of his appeal to others, and today was no exception. He looked tired. Shattered, in fact. He lowered his tall frame into a chair and looked up with a smile at the waitress who instantly approached him. Interesting that in a room packed full of patrons and potential tips, she made a beeline for Keaton, Honor thought with an ironic smile. She realized she was using the thumb of her left hand to twirl her engagement ring back and forth, like she always did when she was slightly anxious about something, and forced herself to stop.

There was an air of something different about him tonight that she couldn't quite put her finger on, but then she got it. He was dressed far too casually. Keaton Richmond was the kind of man who never dressed down—not even for a picnic. Not that they'd made a habit of casual al fresco dining, she conceded. But the leather jacket draped over his shoulders looked well worn and soft, as if he'd owned it for years. She didn't remember seeing it on him ever before, but then again, as they didn't live together, it wasn't as if she was privy to everything he had in his wardrobe.

He lifted his head and scanned the room, his eyes skimming past her before doubling back to give her another look. She smiled at him. He didn't smile back initially, but then his lips curved into a half smile that sent a bolt of longing straight to her core. She straightened and was about to move toward him, but he turned his head and continued to survey the room before focusing his attention to the bar snacks menu standing on his table.

So, he was playing a game now, was he? Pretending he didn't even know her. Honor didn't know whether to be annoyed or intrigued. Maybe he'd actually listened the last time they'd had a discussion about where their relationship was heading. Goodness knew they hadn't had sex in months and, even then, it had been an outlet rather than an expression of devotion. She'd begun to wonder if all her hopes and dreams for her future were on the road to being dashed.

Keaton had been noncommittal when she'd suggested they spice things up in the bedroom, maybe even move in together before the wedding, for which they had yet to set a date. This limbo they'd allowed themselves to fall into had begun to niggle at her in ways it shouldn't have. She and Keaton had worked together at his family's firm since she'd joined it five years ago, and they'd begun to date two years ago. They'd gotten engaged eighteen months later.

It had hardly been the romance of the century, but then again, Honor had told herself she was never looking for romance. Look at where that had gotten her mom. No, when she'd won her role at Richmond Developments, she'd set her sights on the top of their corporate ladder, and if marrying the CEO's son would get her there faster, then she was prepared to do even that to reach her goal. Besides, it wasn't as if she didn't like or respect Keaton. They just needed to rekindle the spark now and then.

But games weren't his style.

So why was he playing one now?

It intrigued her on a level that made her want to play along and see exactly where this was headed. The waitress brought a tall lager over to Keaton's table. Again, he surprised her. She'd never known Keaton to drink beer. Not even on a hot summer's day. She continued to observe him as he lifted the frosted glass to his lips and tipped it up, taking long, steady gulps. She watched the muscles of his throat work as he swallowed, saw the moisture glistening on his lips as he set the glass down again. Felt the visceral tug of desire that pulled hard inside her as he licked his lips. He looked up again. Caught her eye.

He looked surprised to find her still staring at him, and he gave her that half smile again. Honor felt her nipples tighten into hard nubs that rubbed against the lace of her demi-cup bra. Wow. She couldn't remember when she'd felt this uncontrollably drawn to him. It was time to stop playing games and time to act. Honor reached into her clutch and extracted one of the two room key cards she'd been given at check-in and palmed it in her hand.

The woman sashayed across the room; there was no other way to describe it. She was dressed in a form-fitting black cocktail dress with very interesting cut-outs at the waist that fit as if it had been made for her. Logan watched as she determinedly made her way through the crowd. Several people tried to draw her into conversation, but she smoothly turned each attempt aside, her focus solely on him.

He'd had no sleep on the twelve-plus-hour flight that had left his home city of Auckland, New Zealand, at nine last night. On arrival in Los Angeles, he'd caught a connecting flight up to Seattle. Severely jet-lagged and trying desperately to adjust to a time zone that was twenty hours behind his own, he'd forced himself to go for a walk and stay awake on arrival. Now all he craved was a cold beer, a light meal and bed. He wasn't looking for polite conversation or company, but it looked as though company was coming, whether he wanted it or not.

And, he had to admit, she was a darn fine-looking woman. Her blond hair was long and thick and swept over one shoulder, the ends of it just reaching her breasts. Breasts he could see a glimpse of through the keyhole at the front of her dress. The garment was sophisticated and sexy. Even so, he'd bet it would look better off. Like on the floor of his hotel room.

Logan shook his head. *Nope, nope, nope.* He wasn't here for any of that. He was here to find his identity, however lame that sounded. Hell, he was a grown, thirty-four-year-old man. If he didn't know who he was by now, he was probably making a mess of his life. But he'd been confident he knew exactly who he was—right up until he'd found that box tucked away in the back of his late mom's wardrobe when he was clearing her house for sale. Everyone joked about finding skeletons in a closet after someone had passed away. He hadn't expected to be the skeleton.

A sense of frustration beat at the back of his mind. He'd spent his whole life calling Alison Parker Mom. But, as it turned out, she wasn't his mother. And now he was here in the United States to find the people who were his real parents and hoping like hell they'd accept him.

In his moment of reverie, the stunning creature in the killer black dress had drawn up closer to him. He felt her presence before he became fully aware of her intentions. Her hand caught his chin and tilted his face up to hers and then, quite shockingly, she kissed him.

At first Logan didn't respond—in fact, his over-tired brain was in such a state of disbelief he couldn't

even react, but then instinct won over. The silky soft-
ness of her lips on his sent every nerve in his body into
screaming overload. His eyes slid closed, and he focused solely on the sensation of her mouth on his. On
the feel of her tantalizing lips, and then on the thrill-
ing texture of her tongue as she licked the seam of his
mouth. All sound around them faded into nothing. All
he could hear was the pounding of his blood through
his veins as his heart rate went into double time. All he
could smell was the sultry, spicy hint of her fragrance.

And then it was over. She was moving away. His
eyes flicked open. He went to speak, but she put one
forefinger against his lips.

"Don't say a word, lover. Room 6035. Meet me upstairs in ten minutes."

With that, she pressed a key card into his palm and
walked away. He watched in stunned amazement as
she continued out into the foyer and toward the elevator bank. Logan's fingers closed tight around the key
card. There was no way in hell he was going to follow
her upstairs. No way. Therein lay trouble for certain.
He'd be drugged, have organs stolen and wake up in a
bath packed with ice.

Or he'd have the best freaking night of his entire life.

The sliders and fries he'd ordered arrived, together
with a second beer. He eyed them both before rapidly
consuming the sliders and leaving the beer. No more
alcohol for him. He needed a clear head. He flicked
a glance at his watch. Ten minutes was up. He could
still feel her lips on his own. Before he even realized
he had reached a decision, Logan left a handful of bills

on the table and was on his feet and walking toward the elevators.

He got out on the sixth floor and walked down the corridor, hesitating a moment outside room 6035. Then he raised the key card to the reader at the door. The light went green, and he stepped inside. The room was dimly lit, but he had no difficulty finding the enticing creature who'd kissed him senseless in the bar and then made him break with every ounce of common sense he'd ever possessed. What was he doing, coming to a stranger's hotel room like this?

The woman still wore her dress but had slipped off the killer heels.

"I'm glad you came," she said, walking toward him.

She wound her arms around his neck and reached up to kiss him. Again, that intoxicating blend of her fragrance wafted gently around him, seducing his senses into believing that coming here was a very, very good idea. Logan felt his entire body go up in flames. He wanted her like he'd wanted nothing else. Regret, doubt, confusion—those were all emotions for other people to worry about. Not him. Not now. Not here.

He slid his arms around her waist and pulled her in closer. He didn't feel the need to speak, had no desire to break the spell. He deepened the kiss, letting his tongue slide between her lips and experiencing the stimulating taste that was uniquely this woman. She splayed her hands through his short-cropped hair, her nails gently raking his scalp and sending tiny electric jolts through his entire body.

And then her hands were at his shoulders, sliding

his leather jacket off and tugging at his shirt. He moved
his hands to assist her and broke contact with her lips
for only as long as it took him to tear the shirt up over
his head and away from his overheated flesh. When
their lips met again, he could feel the texture of her
dress against his bare skin, but it wasn't enough. His
hands slid around her back and up to the neckline of
her dress, feeling for the zipper. Success! He caught
the tab between a thumb and forefinger and slowly,
slowly pulled it down.

Logan wrenched his mouth from hers and stepped
away, not wanting to miss a moment of this reveal. At
first the woman looked coy, as if she had suddenly
grown shy, but then as he watched she lifted her hands
to her shoulders and shrugged the top of her dress
loose before letting it slide down her body. His breath
caught in his throat at the sight of her. Honey-gold skin
gleamed in the low light of the hotel room. Her breasts
swelled and spilled over the half cups of her black bra,
and a matching pair of briefs slung high on her hips,
making her legs look as if they went on forever.

He swallowed against the sudden dryness in his
mouth and stepped forward. He started to reach for her,
his hands hesitating only an inch or so from her body.
He could feel the heat pouring off her, a heat matched
by his own body.

"May I?" he asked.

She smiled and ducked her head in a faint nod. It
was all the encouragement he needed. He cupped her
breasts through the lacy bra and thumbed the hard
peaks of her nipples. A tiny gasp fell from the mys-

tery woman's lips, and he captured it in another kiss. He couldn't seem to get enough of her. He eased the straps of her bra off her shoulders and pulled down one cup. Her nipple was a taut bud, and he pinched it lightly between his forefinger and his thumb. He felt the tremor that rippled through her.

"Is that okay?" he asked, his voice little more than a growl.

"More," she begged him.

He repeated the movement, then lowered his head to capture that deep rose-pink nub of flesh with his lips. Again, she shook and sighed. He laved her nipple with his tongue before nipping it lightly.

"More," she demanded now, her hands holding his head to her as if she couldn't bear for him to stop.

And nor could he. Everything about her called to him. Her scent, her taste, her husky pleas that were driving him mad. This all felt like some crazy dream, but he knew he didn't want to wake up. Reality would come back to bite him soon enough. For now, he'd take what he'd been freely offered. And he'd give in return.

Logan backed her against the bed and eased her onto the mattress. He stood between her legs and unbuckled his belt before kicking off his shoes and sliding down his jeans and socks. He didn't trust himself to remove his briefs just yet. Right now he felt as though he was primed and ready to blow. Her slightest touch would be his undoing, and there was no way he was wasting this opportunity. First of all, he was going to make absolutely certain that his mystery woman was with him all the way.

He hooked his fingers in the sides of her panties and slid them down her long, glorious legs. A neat triangle of dark blond hair nestled at the apex of her thighs; he hadn't seen anything quite as sexy in a very long time. Logan lowered himself over her body and reached under her to unsnap the fastening on her bra before easing the confection of lace away from her skin.

"Has anyone ever told you just how exquisitely beautiful you are?" he asked, skimming his hand lightly over the peaks of her breasts before cupping their full weight and squeezing gently.

"Only you," she said on a hoarse whisper, her eyelids fluttering closed as he began to kiss her breasts.

She was writhing beneath him, her hips straining against his. It was all he could do not to unleash his arousal and take her right then, but he was determined to do this right. To ensure she found her pleasure before he even considered taking his. He kissed a warm, wet trail down over her rib cage and to the center of her stomach before drawing a moist line to her belly button with his tongue. He swirled the tip of his tongue in the neat indentation before continuing lower.

He knelt on the floor beside the bed and leaned into her. His nostrils flared on the heated musky scent of her sex, and a pulse of demand bolted through him. He'd never been as completely aware of another human being as he was of this woman. He gently cupped the heated core of her body and felt her push against his palm, striving for more pressure.

"Impatient?" he asked softly.

He took his hand away and blew a stream of air over

her mound and lower still. Her skin there glistened with moisture, and the waves of heat that poured off her almost scorched his fingertips as he let them drift around her entrance.

"You're torturing me," she moaned as he dipped one finger inside her.

"But it's a nice kind of torture, right?"

She clenched tight around him, and for a second all Logan could think about was what that tension would feel like around his penis. But it wasn't his time yet. First, he had to have her trembling with satiation and then he would lift her back up to the heights of physical pleasure all over again. He pressed his nose against her mound and inhaled her deeply, feeling her in every part of him. Then, using his tongue, he began to tease at her clitoris. At first it was just small darts of pressure, but then he began to swirl his tongue around the tight bead of nerve endings. Her breathing grew more rapid, and he looked up at her. Her head was pressed back against the mattress, and a light sheen of perspiration made her chest glisten. A rosy flush was spreading there and her nipples had drawn even more impossibly tight than they'd been before.

Logan eased another finger inside her, stroking her inside and driving her toward what he hoped would be her ultimate satisfaction. He never stopped with the movements of his tongue and then, when he felt she was on the verge of breaking apart, he closed his mouth around her clit and drew on it hard. She fractured beneath him. Her inner muscles squeezed his fingers in a rhythmic pulse that drove him wild. He waited until her body went lax before he moved.

"I didn't know you had that in you," she said in a voice laden with satisfaction.

"Oh, I've got more."

He reached for his trousers, slipped his wallet from his pocket and dragged a condom out. It might be a cliché, but it always paid to be prepared. He quickly slid off his briefs and covered his length with the condom before standing, hooking her knees with his hands and scooting her to the edge of the bed.

"You still okay?" he said.

He'd stop here and now if she said no. It would likely be the toughest thing he'd ever done in his life, but he'd do it.

"Never better," she answered. "Do it. Do me."

He smiled as he positioned himself at her entrance. She was slick with her recent orgasm, and he was inside her in one easy glide. Logan squeezed his eyes shut and held on to the last remnants of his control as he felt her body adjust around him.

"What are you waiting for?" she asked, giving him a squeeze with her internal muscles.

"This," he said as he withdrew and surged back into her again.

At that point everything blurred; there was nothing else in the world except her body and his, joined in the most intimate way a man and woman could be joined. He pumped into her, and she met his every thrust with one of her own. Her breath came in gasps and her hands clutched the bedding beneath her. Logan forced his eyes open, forced himself to look at her, to imprint her image—like this, beneath him, as lost in him as he was lost in her.

He saw that flush creep over her chest again and knew she was close to coming. He had to see her into that sea of pleasure before he could let go. The pulse started deep inside her body, growing stronger with every surge until she peaked, and with it, he reached his climax, too. Again and again, his pleasure rocketed through him. Deep, intense and fiercely satisfying on a primal level.

Logan lowered himself onto her and rolled them both onto their sides. He was still inside her, could still feel her body and his, hearts beating to their perfect rhythm as their pleasure began to ebb and reality began to take its place. The woman raised one hand to his face, tracing his features and looking deep into his eyes.

"I didn't know we could be like this," she said. "That was—no, *you*—were perfect."

"We were perfect," he agreed.

He kissed her then, long and deep and slow. This wasn't the kind of thing he'd ever done before, but they'd both been willing partners and together they'd found a perfection not many had the pleasure of reaching on their first time together.

First and last, he reminded himself. He withdrew from her body and they lay there, their hearts and breathing returning to a normal tempo. He needed to clean up, so he rose from the bed and went through to the bathroom. When he returned, he noticed immediately that she had pulled the covers over herself and fallen fast asleep. While his instincts urged him to join her there, he saw the dismissal in her actions.

She'd had an itch, and he'd scratched it. No harm. No foul.

Logan reached for his clothing and quickly dressed. Leaving her key card on the bedside table, he switched off the light before letting himself out of the room.

He'd never see her again, but he'd never forget her, or this night, for as long as he lived.

Two

Honor woke early the next morning and stretched out in the bed. She reached across for Keaton and was disappointed, but not at all surprised, not to find him there. A large grin spread across her face. Last night had surpassed all her expectations. Even now her body tingled from the pleasure he'd given her.

When she'd suggested spicing things up in their relationship, she'd never expected him to take the suggestion to heart. Oh, sure, she knew he'd heard her when she'd somewhat nervously broached the subject a week or so ago, but when he'd barely even acknowledged her, she had shelved the request in the back of her mind. Keaton was, well, Keaton. Calm, sometimes pedantic and always controlled. Even last night he had remained controlled, but the role play had definitely been something new. Sex between them had always been perfunctory at best. Not to mention infrequent. In fact, she'd begun to fear he was considering breaking off their engagement. Pretending to be a stranger had been a brilliant idea. The way he'd explored her body had been as if it had all been entirely new to him. He'd even put on a bit of a barely discernable foreign accent in the few words they'd exchanged.

She brushed one hand across her breasts, remembering how his touch had felt. How the roughness of his beard had so deliciously abraded her skin. Keaton usually shaved twice a day and never went out with stubble, even though it had looked so darn sexy on him last night. She wondered if she'd be able to convince him to let himself go a little more often. To relax that incredibly strict control he had on himself. Maybe next time, she could play the stranger.

Honor giggled out loud as she considered various situations where she could fulfill the fantasy. The idea of Keaton taking charge and making her an offer she couldn't refuse, as she'd done with him last night, held massive appeal. She squirmed a little against the sheets, regretful that he wasn't here. She had been the recipient of all his attention last night, and she'd unashamedly been the taker. Next time she would show him, using the full extent of her imagination, just how grateful she was that he'd made the effort.

She turned her head and looked at the digital bedside clock. She'd have to get a move on if she was going to make her presentation this morning. She rose from the bed and went through to the bathroom, a new smile pulling at her lips as she spied the empty condom packet in the trash. Honor turned on the shower faucet and stepped under the spray without waiting for it to warm up. Right now, she needed to focus on the conference. Then, later today, she'd be back at work. Back to normal. Back to Keaton.

Anticipation thrummed through her veins. Hopefully last night was the beginning of something new and exciting for them. Her concerns that Keaton had become disengaged from her emotionally had been valid, she was sure of it. But whatever had caused the distance between them no longer seemed to be an issue.

If her worst fears had been realized and he'd broken off their engagement, she had no doubt she would have been expected to leave Richmond Developments. It wouldn't matter how many years she'd worked there. Douglas and Nancy Richmond were fiercely loyal to their children, Keaton and Kristin. Everything they did, they did for them, and it was well-known that Keaton, as the eldest, would assume his father's role as CEO when Douglas retired in two years' time. And it was Honor's hope that she would ascend the ranks to be his second in charge.

Childhood poverty had driven Honor's ambition. Watching her parents tear each other apart with their infidelity and then watching her mother's subsequent spiral into despair and guilt after Honor's dad had walked out for the last time had made Honor determined to never fall into that trap. It was why she had accepted Keaton's proposal. He was steady. There'd be no rapidly flaring emotions that escalated into nasty and vicious arguments. Theirs would be a marriage built on having the same dreams and goals for the future. On living life on a continuous trajectory to success and security.

She'd told herself she was happy with all of that. That it was exactly what she'd wanted all along. But with Keaton reluctant to set a date for the wedding, she'd begun to know fear, and with that fear had come the dreaded sense of insecurity she'd known all too well as a child.

Honor stepped out of the shower and dried herself and reached into her toiletry bag for the solitaire engagement ring Keaton had placed on her finger six months ago. Even his proposal had been one of stolid, pragmatic discussion. Afterward, they'd gone out together to shop for the ring, again, an exercise in restraint, for although he hadn't placed a limit on the price of the ring, he'd eyed it more as an investment piece than a declaration of undying love. She wore the large princess-cut diamond set in platinum with pride. To her it was another example of just how far she'd come.

The ring stuck a little as she pushed it over her knuckle, but with a little coaxing it was back where it belonged. She didn't know what had made her take it off last night after she'd given her room key to Keaton. Somehow it just felt as if it fit the fantasy.

All in all, last night augured well for their future together, she thought as she quickly applied her makeup, brushed her hair into a French knot and slipped into the trouser suit she'd brought to wear today. The severe cut of the cream jacket, teamed with matching tailored trousers, gave her an edge of sophistication blended with a no-nonsense air of business. The beige camisole she wore beneath it had just a hint of antique lace at the neckline to soften the sharp edges. She gave herself one last look in the mirror and nodded. Yes, she'd do.

In the elevator down to the conference, Honor slipped out her phone and keyed a message to Keaton.

I miss you already. Can't wait to see you again. Xx

There was a smile on her face as she pressed Send and put the phone back in her pocket. She didn't expect Keaton to respond. But after last night, it might have been nice to think he would. Before she went into the conference room where she'd be presenting her seminar today, she checked her phone. Nothing. She shouldn't feel disappointed, she told herself as she hooked up her laptop to the system and loaded her PowerPoint display, but it didn't stop her checking her phone once again before the first of the attendees began to wander into the room.

Nothing. Pushing back the biting sense of letdown, Honor focused her thoughts on her notes and began her presentation. She'd have time enough to tell Keaton how much she'd appreciated his actions last night when she got back into the office later today.

Logan rolled over in his bed and stared at the ceiling. Jet lag was an utter bitch. Even though he'd tried to force his body to adjust to the different time zone, he still felt as though he'd need to sleep for a week before he'd feel halfway normal again. But then again, maybe normal was an aberration.

"Too early to be philosophical, mate," he told himself out loud and forced himself from the bed and into the bathroom.

Last night certainly hadn't been normal—not in any way, shape or form. In some respects, he felt a little disappointed in himself. He'd never used another person purely for pleasure before. Not like that. Not without at least getting to know and understand the other person a little better. Hell, he didn't even know his late-night lover's name, even though he knew exactly what drove her into a frenzy—knew exactly where to touch her to make her forget the world and feel pleasure so deeply the edges between where he'd ended and she'd begun had blurred into insignificance.

Would he bump into her again tonight, he wondered? Or this morning, in the lobby downstairs? He studied his reflection in the mirror and shook his head. Man, he looked rough. His beard was growing in, and he needed to attend to that straightaway. He didn't want to bump into anyone looking this disreputable.

After showering, shaving and dressing, Logan headed out to find some breakfast. He had a couple of hours, at best, to get himself adjusted to the time zone and to consider how he was going to accomplish what he'd come here for. Hell, eat breakfast? His gut twisted into a knot and suddenly that was the furthest thing from his mind. Facing his birth mom and dad would be the hardest thing he'd done in his life, knowing they were the people who should have raised him. The people who should have shared each milestone in his life.

Would they understand how, like them, he'd always been drawn to architecture, even as a kid? Would they value his ideals in his work and how he'd built a multi-million-dollar business gutting old buildings and rebuilding them from the inside to create eco-friendly living and work spaces all through Australasia? Would he fit into the family that he'd been born into but never known his entire life?

He had no doubt they'd want proof he was who he said he was. Logan wasn't stupid. He'd done his research. He knew Richmond Developments was on the cutting edge of property development here in the Pacific Northwest. It seemed to Logan that they were in the same kind of business. Except where his parents' company bought old buildings in prime locations, razed them and built new, he preferred to pay homage to the historical character of his projects, preserving and repurposing special features while at the same time bringing them into the twenty-first century. No, his family would likely not immediately welcome him with open arms. Maybe since they were in the same business, they'd think he had ulterior motives. They'd be cautious, and rightly so. They'd need tests done, but eventually his link to them would be proven. And then what?

He wondered, and not for the first time, if he'd have followed his path if he'd been brought up here instead of in New Zealand. Had Alison Parker had any idea of what she was doing when she'd stolen him from his

crib in the nursery at the hospital and taken him to raise
as her own? She couldn't have been in a rational state
of mind—he understood that. She'd given birth to a
stillborn son the same day Logan and his twin brother
were born. The loss had unhinged her. After her death
a couple of months ago, he'd read her old diaries in a
growing state of shock.

It had been clear, even to him, that she must have
been suffering some kind of psychosis after the loss
of her own child. Replacing her dead baby with one
of two living children born to someone else had made
perfect sense to her at the time. As she'd written in her
diary, why should they have two healthy babies when
her own had died? Surely it was only fair that they each
have one? As twisted as it was, he could see how her
grief-stricken mind had justified her actions that day.

And she'd done her best by Logan. When her husband had died on a black ops mission, she'd left the
United States to return to her home country of New
Zealand, where she'd raised Logan as a typical Kiwi
kid. Surfing in the summer, skiing in the winter, he'd
grown up with the best of everything she and her parents could provide, and if anyone asked why he looked
different from his cousins, with his dark blond hair,
fair skin and pale gray eyes, it was explained that he
resembled his father. He was family and had always
felt accepted as such.

But even so, Logan had always felt a lingering sense
of disconnection, too, as if he didn't quite belong. And
after finding that box with his mom's old diaries and
his original baby ID bracelet with his real name on it

together with the one of her dead son, he'd finally understood why. He hadn't told anyone back at home the real reason for his trip to America. They all thought he was here to expand Parker Construction's business interests. And maybe, if everything went well, he would.

The time to make his way to the Richmond Developments headquarters came around all too quickly. After his walk, Logan returned to the hotel to gather his briefcase and went downstairs to summon a cab. At Richmond Tower, Logan checked his appearance in the shiny reflective walls of the elevator and approved the professional look he'd gone for to strike just the right note. In his briefcase were scanned copies of Alison's diaries and the baby bracelets. He'd arranged this meeting with his birth father on the pretext of discussing a business opportunity with him. And it wasn't a complete lie. Logan strongly believed that Richmond Developments was missing a very important niche in the market. The world was looking to repurpose more and more, and conserving old buildings and their histories was the wave of the future. People needed something to be grounded in—as he well knew.

The elevator doors slid open onto a plush reception area. The two women at the front desk both looked up and smiled at him. But behind the smiles, there was confusion, also. The younger of the two stood up.

"Mr. Richmond?"

"I'm Logan Parker to see Mr. Douglas Richmond," Logan said firmly.

"You're Mr. Parker," she said in a confused tone of voice.

The other receptionist tugged on her arm and muttered something, and the younger woman forced a smile to her face. "I'll put a call through."

Logan had discovered he had a twin and that his twin worked here in the family business. He'd hoped that by coming here and meeting his family in their place of work that it would dilute what could be a somewhat fraught reunion. What he hadn't really stopped to consider was the interest there might be in his twin's mirror image suddenly turning up unexpectedly.

"A Mr. Parker is here to see Mr. Richmond," she said discreetly. "Yes, sir. I'll bring him through myself."

She rose from her chair and walked up to Logan. "Please come with me, Mr. Parker."

He followed her down a long corridor, past an openplan office area where people were industriously busy at their workstations. When the receptionist reached a set of large wooden double doors, she knocked before swinging them both open.

"Mr. Parker to see you, sir," she announced before turning back to Logan. "Go on in." She gestured for him to go inside.

"Thank you."

Logan stepped through the doorway and felt as if he'd entered the lion's den. He squared his shoulders. Whatever happened next would determine the course for the rest of his life.

Three

An older man rose from his executive chair behind a large mahogany desk. Despite his tan, his face paled visibly.

"Keaton? What are you doing?"

"No, sir, I'm Logan Parker."

The older man's face paled visibly.

"Who the hell are you?" he demanded, obviously defaulting to anger.

"As I said, I'm Logan Parker. Although you may remember me by another name," Logan said firmly as he stepped forward and offered his hand.

"Another name? Explain yourself."

"I was born Kane Douglas Richmond," Logan said as calmly as he was able.

"That can't be. Our son disappeared more than thirty years ago. Isn't that right, Nancy?"

When he first walked in, Logan hadn't seen the woman standing by the floor-to-ceiling windows of the large corner office. He turned to face her and heard her sharply indrawn breath.

"Kane? Douglas, could it be…?"

Her knees buckled slightly as she looked at him, and she put a hand out to the chair beside her to steady herself. Tears began to roll down her face and she shook as she reached out a hand.

"Kane. Oh my goodness. Douglas, it's him. It's our baby boy come back to us after all these years."

Douglas Richmond moved quickly from behind his desk and guided his wife into a chair before turning to face Logan.

"What's the meaning of this? Who are you?" he demanded again.

"Sir, I'm sorry. I probably should have told you who I was ahead of our meeting, but I wasn't sure you'd see me if I claimed to be the son who was stolen from you decades ago."

"And that's what you're claiming?"

"Douglas, can't you see it? He's identical to Keaton," Nancy said, reaching up and grasping hold of her husband's hand. "It has to be Kane. Our firstborn."

But Douglas Richmond was determined not to be convinced. "I understood you requested this meeting to discuss business. What do you really want from us?"

"Yes, I did," Logan admitted. "And that's something I'd still like to talk over with you. But first, I would like to show you these. I can understand that you're both shocked—I was, too, when I discovered my true identity."

Logan placed his briefcase on a chair and opened it. He took out the diary copies and the ID bracelets from the hospital and placed them on his father's desk.

"These belonged to the woman who raised me. Please, look at them at your leisure. If you prefer, I can leave them with you now and return at a later time."

It was clear his father and mother were completely shell-shocked by his arrival. To be totally honest, he was, too. Looking at his dad was like entering a time machine—one that projected him thirty years ahead. And his mom, too. He had her coloring—the exact same shade of pale gray eyes. Despite their obvious distress at his sudden appearance in their lives, he could feel a tenuous connection with them already. One born of recognition, of blood. Even so, perhaps it was a good time to leave. To let them absorb the information he'd brought with him.

"I can see my arrival here has unsettled you both. Let me give you some time." He dropped his business card on the diaries. "You can reach me on my mobile number. I'll wait at my hotel for your call."

He turned toward the door.

"No, don't go!" Nancy cried out and struggled to her feet.

She came across the carpeted floor, stopped directly in front of him and reached her hands up to his face, cupping his cheeks.

"Nancy, you can't be sure it's him," Douglas said cautiously.

"Don't you dare tell me I don't know my own son," she said fiercely, never taking her eyes off Logan for a second. "This is my boy. You grew within my body. I birthed you, held you, nursed you and then you were stolen from me. But now you're returned to us, and our family is once again complete."

Logan didn't know what to do or say, but his silence didn't deter Nancy.

"Douglas, call in Keaton and Kristin. They need to meet him. They need to see their brother."

To Logan's surprise, his father did just that. He placed two calls in quick succession requesting that his two other children come immediately to his office.

"Take a seat, young man. I'm sure we won't have to wait long," Douglas said gruffly before resuming his seat behind the desk. He didn't take his eyes off Logan for a minute.

Logan sat and remained still. Nancy had taken the chair next to him. Both his parents kept staring at him, his mother with a look of sheer wonder on her face, his father with disbelief. It couldn't have been more than two minutes before there was a peremptory knock at the door and another man walked in. Logan rose and turned to face the newcomer.

"What the hell is going on?" his mirror image asked with a look of shock on his face.

Logan stared at his twin brother. His identical twin. It was uncanny staring at another person who was the spitting image of yourself. They even had the same haircut.

"Keaton, meet your brother, Kane, or, as he's known, Logan Parker," Nancy said in a slightly unsteady voice.

"I don't know who this impostor is, but I don't have a brother," Keaton said firmly.

Logan felt the words as though they were a physical blow. All his life he'd wanted siblings. Now that he'd discovered he had two, it had become all the more important to him that they believe he was who he said he was—their long-lost brother.

"If it's any consolation," Logan said, "until very recently I had no idea you existed, either."

There was a commotion at the door, and a young woman came in. Probably his sister, judging by her resemblance to Nancy.

"What's going on? Who's this?" she said before coming to an abrupt halt as she saw her brother standing there with his double.

"Kristin, this is your brother," Nancy said. "Your other brother."

"He can't be. My other brother is dead."

"I can assure you, I'm very much alive," Logan replied.

"How can that be possible?" Kristin said, turning on her mom. "You told me when I was little that he was dead."

"What your mother said was that your brother was gone. The rest was your own interpretation," Douglas said gruffly. "Obviously there is a strong resemblance—"

"Resemblances mean nothing," Keaton said insistently and took a step closer to Logan. "I don't know who the heck you are, but you have a nerve coming here and trying to pull this off. How much money do you want?"

Logan snorted. "Money? I have plenty of money. What I don't have, and what I've been cheated of my entire life, is my family."

"So, you thought you'd appropriate ours?" Kristin said snidely.

Logan reached for the hospital ID tag he'd put on his father's desk. "If I was an impostor, would I have this?"

Kristin took one of the tiny bracelets. "Anyone could fake this."

Logan firmed his lips into a straight line. This wasn't turning into the warm family reunion he'd hoped for.

"Look, I'll do whatever it takes to prove I am who I believe I am." Logan stared back at Keaton. "Just tell me where and when I need to be at the lab for the DNA test, and I'll be there."

"You're very confident of your claim," Keaton said.

"I'm not in the habit of lying or misleading people," Logan answered firmly. "Look, until my mother—at least, the woman who raised me—died recently, I always believed that she and her late husband were my parents, even though I didn't look much like either of them. Mum met her husband when he was stationed at Antarctica with the joint forces support force. She was a New Zealand nurse stationed there, too. She followed him to the US and they married here. It was only after she passed away that I found these." He gestured to the diary copies on the desk. "And the ID bracelets."

"To the best of my knowledge, Alison Parker learned her husband had been killed on deployment and went into labor with her own son. He was still-born. I can only surmise that her grief, doubled, drove her over the edge. She states in her diary that while the nursing staff were doing a shift changeover, there was an emergency in another room and the nursery was left unattended for a brief time. She entered the nursery from the maternity ward where she'd just been discharged and simply lifted me from my crib, hid me in her overnight bag and took me home.

"She later traveled from Seattle to Los Angeles and applied for a passport for me in her dead child's name at the New Zealand consulate. The military helped with her return to New Zealand on compassionate grounds. And, because she was known to have been pregnant, no one thought anything of the fact that she had a baby with her. She'd come to the US on her New Zealand passport, which was in her maiden name. I can only assume that any attempt to trace her was thrown off by that."

Nancy stiffened in her chair. "That definitely explains it. Remember, Douglas, the hospital staff and police virtually ripped the hospital apart looking for Kane. They investigated everyone who'd been in the hospital during the time he was born and there was one woman they'd had difficulty tracing but they'd excluded her from the investigation because when they found her on security tapes she wasn't carrying a baby, only a bag." She swallowed a sob back. "And you were in that bag."

Before anyone could say anything else, there was another knock at the office door.

"I'm sorry I'm late, everyone. I just got back into wor—"

All eyes turned to the woman who'd just come into the office. A woman Logan recognized instantly. His late-night lover. But she wasn't the warm, sexy creature who'd approached and kissed him then invited him up to her room. Instead, she was a cool, remote corporate type—wearing an enormous diamond on the ring finger of her left hand.

And, as she looked from his brother to him, he saw the exact moment that she realized exactly whom she'd propositioned last night.

"Keaton? What's going on?"

Logan watched as she crossed the office to stand at his brother's side.

"That's what we'd all like to know. This guy claims to be my twin brother."

Honor fought the urge to flee. This couldn't be happening. There couldn't be two Keatons, and the longer she stood here the more strongly the truth reverberated through her. She'd slept with a stranger. Sure, he'd looked like her fiancé, but no matter which way she looked at it, she'd cheated on Keaton. And not just cheated, but cheated on him with *his brother*.

The bitter taste of bile flooded her mouth and she swallowed it back. This couldn't be happening. Fidelity was her line in the sand. She'd seen exactly what unfaithfulness could do to a family and she'd vowed, always, to be faithful. And yet somehow, she'd made the most monumental mistake of her entire life.

Douglas reached across the desk and grabbed one of the duplicate diaries stacked there.

"I suppose I'd better read these. In the meantime, Nancy, could you look into how we can have DNA testing expedited?"

"Yes, dear, I'll check on it right away." She started toward the door but paused and turned back to Logan.

Honor watched as her future mother-in-law took the hand of the man with whom Honor had committed her biggest mistake. The man who, with only a few words, could destroy her carefully, painstakingly constructed future. Under the bright office lights, a myriad of diamonds glinted on Nancy's fingers, each one a gift from her husband and a testament to his love for her. Honor began to worry at her own diamond ring with her thumb. How on earth was she going to work through this?

Nancy leaned closer to the newcomer and said, "Don't worry, my son. It'll work out. I know in my heart you're telling the truth. A mother always knows."

Honor watched as Nancy went through the door to her connecting office. It had always amazed Honor that Nancy and Douglas believed in working closely together even after all this time. It had added to her sense of security knowing that even with all life had thrown at them thirty-four years ago with their first-born being kidnapped, her future in-laws continued to stand strong together. It was what she'd always hoped for, for herself and Keaton. And, while she wasn't on his management level yet, she was working steadily toward it. When Douglas and Nancy retired, she and Keaton would be the power couple here at Richmond Developments. And when that happened, she'd be living her dream.

But only if the truth of what she did last night was never revealed.

Something stabbed sharply in her chest. How could she keep what she'd done a secret? Even knowing it would destroy her relationship with Keaton and likely see her have to find another position elsewhere, she knew, deep down, that she ought to come clean. And what of the stranger? Would he keep their one night of illicit passion secret, or was he the kind of man who'd use their secret to gain leverage with the Richmond family?

Right now, she had no way of knowing what kind of person he was. Obviously, she knew he was a talented and generous lover, but what was he like as a man? He'd accepted her offer to come up to her room without a backward glance. Having sex with a complete and utter stranger didn't really do much to recommend him, but then again, she'd been complicit in that. Forget that she thought she'd been making love with the man she'd pledged to marry. As Keaton's fiancée, she should have known all along that this man was not the same person.

But didn't you see the differences and choose to ignore them? a little voice that sounded horribly like her mother's asked from the back of her mind. *You think you're so squeaky clean, but you're no different from me after all.*

Honor clamped down on the thought immediately. Maybe she was all wrong here. Maybe it had been Keaton at the hotel last night. After all, she'd invited him to come along, had told him how important it was to her to be nominated for the award she'd won. And he'd known she wanted to spice things up between them. Even though she knew she was grasping at straws, she turned to him.

"Keaton, can I ask you something?" she murmured in his ear.

"Sure." He looked at her and his direct, pale gray eyes felt as if they were boring into the recesses of her soul—as if he could see the truth of her actions last night.

She forced a smile and leaned in to ask, "Where were you last night?"

"I told you, I had a business dinner," he said. "I'm sorry I couldn't be there for you to celebrate your win. Congratulations, by the way. We can do dinner tonight, and you can tell me all about it. Let's get through this mess first."

Honor looked past Keaton's shoulder at her secret lover, who was staring straight back at her. A shiver rippled through her. Fear? Or was it something else?

"Honor?" Keaton prompted.

"Yes," she said, gathering her wits about her. What had he just said to her? Oh yes. "That would be lovely. I'll look forward to it."

Douglas spoke again. "Kristin, could you get Stella to bring in some strong, hot coffee for us? I think we all need something bracing."

"Whiskey might be more in order," she grumbled before stepping out of the office.

"Keaton, you haven't introduced your fiancée to Mr. Parker yet," Douglas said.

Honor saw the stranger's head jerk a little, as if he'd just received an electric shock. He looked from her to Keaton and back again. Confusion and what had to be a million questions vied for supremacy in his eyes. She couldn't hold his gaze. Couldn't face the damnation she knew she'd see there if she looked at him for too long. Beside her, Keaton stiffened before making the introduction.

"Honor, this, apparently, is my long-lost twin brother, Kane, also known as Logan Parker. Parker, please meet my fiancée, Honor Gould."

Logan stepped forward and offered Honor his hand. "Pleased to meet you, Ms. Gould."

Honor slowly let go of the breath she'd been holding. She'd half expected him to admit that he'd already met her, but it appeared he was happy to pretend he hadn't. Hadn't met her, hadn't kissed her, hadn't touched her body so intimately that she was in danger of flaring into a plume of smoke at the sheer memory of what he'd done to her, with her.

But she could see the questions in his eyes, and she knew she'd have to face them down—sooner rather than later. Her mind working overtime, she admitted to herself it would need to be sooner. She couldn't risk him disclosing to Keaton what they'd done. At least with the way Keaton had been bristling around Logan, they were hardly likely to be sharing close conversation any time soon. She took his hand, schooling herself to remain calm, but she hadn't anticipated the electricity that sizzled through her palm at his touch.

"And you too, Mr. Parker," she finally managed to say through stiff lips. "Your arrival here is quite a surprise."

As if that wasn't the biggest understatement of her life.

"I can imagine," Logan Parker replied.

Was that a twinkle in his eye? Did he find this situation funny? A bolt of anger shot through her. How dare he? He had to realize that she'd made an innocent mistake, even if what had transpired next had been anything but innocent. She had to get him on his own to clarify this situation and ensure that he would keep what they'd done strictly between them.

But could she trust him?

Four

The next hour passed painfully slowly. Somehow Nancy used the Richmond influence to have a private lab technician come directly to the office. The man swabbed Douglas and Nancy, then Keaton and Logan. It seemed that when big money talked, people moved and moved fast.

After the technician had left, Honor excused herself.

"I'm sorry, I have an off-site client meeting in half an hour. I really need to get going. I hope you'll excuse me."

Nancy looked up and smiled. "Of course, Honor. I was thinking we should have a family dinner back at the house tonight. Take the opportunity to get to know Logan a little better."

"Oh, I'm sorry, Keaton and I have other plans for

tonight." She looked across to her fiancé. "Unless you want to—"

"Yes, Mom, we do. Neither of us will be able to make it. Perhaps some other time," Keaton added, overriding the suggestion Honor was clearly about to make that they change their plans.

Logan had no doubt that Keaton was hoping "some other time" would never happen. Hostility poured off his brother in waves. He could understand it. For thirty-four years, Keaton had been the much-loved only son of his parents. Now he had competition. Kristin appeared to be aloof, too. She hadn't exhibited any of the curiosity he knew he himself would have displayed in the same situation. He might have sought his family and found them, but along the way he'd also discovered a whole pile of doubt.

Obviously, a family like the Richmonds would need to be careful. They'd built an empire on very tight-knit foundations. It only made sense that they'd close ranks to protect it. But there'd been no doubting the recognition and joy on Nancy's face. Douglas, too, seemed less reticent than his children when it came to Logan.

He sat back in his chair. It would take time to prove it, but he had every confidence he had as much right to be here as any of them.

And then there was the conundrum of the intriguing Honor Gould. Logan watched her talking to his brother by the windows that looked out over the water. It was obvious that she'd been shocked to discover she'd slept with the wrong twin, but what did that say about her relationship with Keaton? Surely she must have seen that while they might look the same, their similarities ended with that. From what Logan could tell, his brother was a very tightly reined-in person emotionally. Was he equally as tightly reined in when it came to intimacy?

He didn't like what the thought of his brother and Honor being intimate did to him—and especially didn't like the powerful surge of possessiveness that swept through him. Logan shook his head slightly. Whatever, it was none of his business. If Honor wanted to pretend they'd never met before, he was good with that. At least for now. But he still felt the pull of attraction between them, and he had no doubt that would become very uncomfortable before long. He hadn't missed the engagement ring on her finger this morning, either. The ring that definitely hadn't been there when he'd gone to her room last night.

Man, last night. He fought back the groan of desire that threatened to pour out of him. Yeah, that would go down well right now—*not*. He had to keep his mind off Honor Gould, but it was going to be damn hard when she was right here in the room. Didn't she mention she had some off-site visit she needed to be at? And yet, all of a sudden she didn't appear to be in a hurry to leave after all. She was still standing and talking with Keaton, whispering and gesturing and occasionally looking Logan's way. But then, thank goodness, she began to move toward the door.

There was no kiss or hug between her and Keaton as she departed. *Interesting.* They might be engaged, but there didn't appear to be any real closeness between them. In fact, Logan was willing to wager that he had been closer to Honor last night than his brother had been in a very long time.

Stop it, he told himself. *You're grasping at straws. Competing with a brother you never knew you had until a couple of months ago over the woman he's engaged to.* As if that wasn't the most cynical thing of all. He didn't know Honor—not what made her tick, what her favorite breakfast was, what music she enjoyed, the books she liked. Nor did he know his brother. Maybe beneath that stuffed-shirt, cold exterior, Keaton was indeed a warm-blooded male.

Logan caught his brother's eye and gave him a half smile of acknowledgment, but Keaton's expression didn't change. In fact, he turned away and with a muttered excuse to his father departed soon after Honor. Which left Kristin and his parents.

He decided it was time to get to know his sister a little better.

"So, Kristin—or do I call you Krissie?"

"Kristin. I loathe being called Krissie." Her response was succinct and laced with animosity.

"Right, duly noted. When I did a little research into the company before coming here, I saw that you're chief financial officer and heavily involved in the leasing side of the business—"

"You researched us? Kind of creepy, don't you think?"

"And you haven't googled me since you learned of my existence?"

He was taking a punt, but he suspected she had. If

not when he'd seen her pull her phone out of her pocket while the lab tech was here, then definitely when she'd left the office to request the coffee.

She had the grace to look shamefaced. "I might have."

"Were you being creepy, or merely looking to be informed about who you were dealing with?"

"Touché," Douglas commented with a chuckle. "He has you there, Kristin."

She looked annoyed, and Logan attempted to put out the fire of discontent that was building in her eyes.

"I get it. I hate walking into any situation with my eyes shut. And, yes, I admit that I probably should have had my lawyers approach the family with my claim." He shook his head. "Not that I'm making any claim. I just wanted to find my family. My real family. The people I have a connection with that goes beyond today. The woman who brought me up loved me, and her family loved me as if I was their own, but I always knew I was different. Can you imagine what that was like?"

He watched Kristin's gaze soften and heard the muffled sound of compassion that came from Nancy. He waited a couple of beats, letting his words sink in.

"So you can understand my need to find out what I could when I discovered the diaries. I don't expect you all to include me in your lives. But obviously I would like it if we could have some crossover, whether that be on a personal or business level."

"Business? You were serious about that? Or was that just the ruse you used to get in to see Mom and Dad this morning?"

"It's no ruse. If you looked me up online, you'll know I'm an experienced architect and I specialize in the repurposing and renovation of old buildings."

"Well, if you looked us up online, you'll know we specialize in pulling old buildings down."

He laughed at the belligerence in his sister's tone and found a growing respect for her. She didn't back down. He liked that.

"And that's where I think you're missing an opportunity."

"Tell me more," Douglas said, leaning forward and resting his elbows on his desk.

The next several hours passed in a blur of conversation as they discussed the pros and cons of their respective businesses. Toward the end of the afternoon, Douglas leaned back in his chair and smiled.

"If you are who you say you are and you hadn't been taken from us, I wonder where Richmond Developments would be now."

"Oh, come on, Dad. We don't even know for certain that he's your son," Kristin said, obviously not ready to let go of her reluctance to accept Logan as her brother.

"Kristin, I think the sooner you come to terms with the fact our family dynamic may be about to change, the better."

"Well, it's hardly going to change for me, is it? After all, you only ever wanted Keaton, as your eldest living son, at the helm when you retire. So is that going to be Logan now?"

Logan looked from his birth father to his sister in shock. He certainly hadn't expected that. Nor, to be

honest, did he want it. At the very least, he had no right
to intrude on Keaton's position both as Douglas's son
and within the company hierarchy.

"You know my wishes," Douglas said severely. "And
I'll thank you not to try and cause trouble."

"Dad, stop treating me like I'm five years old."

"Then stop behaving like you are."

Kristin looked at father, hurt clear on her features. "I think I'll go back to my office now."

And without saying another word, she left.

"I'm sorry you had to witness that," Douglas said
with a wry twist to his mouth. "Kristin tends to let her
emotions get the better of her."

"Now, Doug, that's not entirely fair. You bait her,"
Nancy objected.

"And she needs to learn that sometimes you have to
lead with your head, not your heart."

Logan watched the interplay between his parents.
Would Nancy continue to stand up to Douglas? No, it
was clear she was about to concede the point.

"Looks like it's just the three of us left," Nancy
commented. "Shall we head back to the house early?
Logan, perhaps you'd like to stay with us until you find
a place of your own?"

"I have my room at the hotel," Logan remonstrated.
"I'm happy to stay there for now. Besides, I plan on
returning to New Zealand, not settling down here."

"No," Nancy cried out. "I haven't had you for the
past thirty-four years. You can't go back so soon."

"Well, I'm not going back immediately, but eventually. I do have a company to run."

"Possibly two," Douglas said enigmatically before rising from his chair. "But for now, you'll at least come home for dinner, won't you?"

Logan looked from his father to his mother. "Yes, I'd like that. Thank you."

He still had so many questions he wanted to ask. So many answers he sought. He might as well continue the conversation tonight, even if his siblings weren't going to be there. *Or Honor*, the voice at the back of his mind pointed out. He quashed the thought before it could take flight. For now, he would have to be satisfied with what he had right here in front of him. After all, hadn't that been his goal in coming here all along?

But no matter what he told himself, his body remembered his brother's fiancée with an ache that wouldn't go away.

Honor was on tenterhooks, waiting for Keaton to arrive at her apartment. She double-checked the table setting, lit the tall candles in their holders and tweaked the blooms she'd picked up from Pike Place Market on the way home from work and arranged in the crystal bowl she'd found in a thrift shop a few months back.

Everything looked perfect. On the surface, at least. But she couldn't quite shake the feeling that life as she knew it was about to change irrevocably. It terrified her. One aberration could rip apart her carefully planned life and destroy any chance of the future she had worked so hard for all her life.

She heard the door buzz. Keaton must have arrived. He was the only person on her "do not announce" list she'd left with the concierge downstairs. She flew across the room, pulled open the door and embraced Keaton.

"I have missed you so much," she said on a rush of air.

He extracted himself from her embrace. "Honor, we were together this morning."

"But not just the two of us. I feel like we never have time for each other anymore." At the quizzical expression on his face, she realized she was probably saying too much, too soon. "I'm sorry. It's been a heck of a day. Come inside and sit down. Can I get you a drink?"

"Sure. I'll open this for us, shall I?" Keaton showed her the bottle of merlot he'd brought and went through to the living room.

Honor glanced at the wine label and grimaced slightly as she saw it was imported from New Zealand. Seemed there was an awful lot coming from New Zealand right now.

"Something smells good."

"Lasagna," she answered. "The merlot will be perfect with it."

She got two glasses from the kitchen and brought them through to the living room. Keaton opened the bottle and poured them each a glass. He handed her one, and she snuggled in beside him on the couch.

"Don't you wish we could do this every night after work?" she probed.

He'd never responded to her suggestion that they move in together. Instead he'd been evasive and turned their discussion back to an issue they'd been having with a bulk supplier for one of their commercial developers at the time. Honor loved Keaton, she really did, and admired his work ethic like nothing else, but his ability to avoid answering a straight question with a straight answer drove her slightly crazy.

"I can see where it will have its benefits," he agreed before dropping a kiss onto the tip of her nose.

She pulled a face. "That's no way to say a proper hello to the woman you're going to marry," she said before reaching up to turn his face to hers and kissing him.

She put everything she had into the kiss. All her guilt about last night, all her hope that she hadn't destroyed the now-tenuous link between herself and Keaton. He didn't respond at first, and she wondered if she'd pushed him too hard. Keaton was the kind of man who liked to initiate things. It had never really bothered her that much. But now, it lit a wick on her anger.

Why didn't he want to take her and ravish her? They'd been apart for a few days while she'd been at the conference and then they'd had the upheaval of Logan Parker turning up. Surely he should be turning to her for comfort. Wasn't that what couples did in times of stress and strife? But even as she kissed him, she felt his restraint. Sure, he went through the motions, but where was the passion?

Had it ever been there?

She hated that she was now second-guessing herself about a relationship she was prepared to stake her future on. Or at least she had been until she'd realized she'd slept with the wrong brother. No! She couldn't think like that. She had honestly believed that she'd been with Keaton, hadn't she? She'd honestly believed that her staid, upright, workaholic fiancé had dressed in clothing she hadn't recognized and spoken in a different accent to indulge in role play and put a bit of fun in their relationship.

Honor pulled away from Keaton and took a sip of her wine. Her hand shook a little as she raised the glass to her mouth. Not because of how he'd kissed her, but because she'd realized that she *had* noticed things were off about Logan Parker and that she'd chosen to ignore them, even though common sense told her that Keaton would never have done that.

And now she'd been unfaithful to him. It was more than she could contemplate. For all that she'd set herself on a pedestal so much higher than her mother, she was cut from the same cloth. The right thing to do would be to admit her awful mistake to Keaton, return his ring and step down from her position at Richmond Developments. But if she did that, she'd lose everything.

Keaton sighed, and she looked up at him in concern. He never sighed. Never expressed weakness. Ever.

"Are you okay? It's been a heck of a day, right?" she asked him.

"That's one way of putting it. Do you think he's genuine?"

"Who? Logan?"

"I didn't have any other brothers come back from the dead today, so, yeah, Logan."

She hesitated. She'd thought him real enough last

night. "Actually, yes, I do think he's genuine. Why did you think he was dead?"

Keaton shook his head slowly. "I don't really know. I guess that the few times I can ever remember Mom and Dad talking about him, they called him their lost son. As a child I assumed that meant he was dead. And because losing him had caused them so much obvious pain, I never asked them any more questions about him. They only ever had the one photo of the both of us from when we were born, before he was abducted."

"Do they still have the photo?"

"Yeah, Mom keeps it in their bedroom, on her dresser, so she can see it every day. I used to think it was morbid, but I guess she never lost hope that he'd come home one day."

"And now he has."

"We don't know that for sure," Keaton said defensively, then sighed again. "But, yeah, I guess the writing is on the wall. You know, I feel like I've spent my entire life trying to make up for my brother's absence. Trying to be better than just one son for my parents. Working my ass off so that they didn't miss him so much and believing I could fill every gap left behind because he wasn't there. Seems I was wrong about that."

"Oh, Keaton. That's not true. Your parents adore you. They know how hard you work, and they appreciate everything you do. Everything you are. How could they not?"

He gave her a sad half smile, one so similar to Logan's that she felt a piercing shaft of compassion mixed with pain and regret puncture her heart. Poor Keaton. She'd never stopped to consider how he saw over-achievement as the only possible option. After all, she was very similar herself. They had goals and they went for them. And, underneath it all, he was still that man looking for approval and acceptance from his parents.

The realization was shocking.

And now his position was on the verge of being usurped by his own twin. She could totally understand how unsettling that must be for him. And she knew equally as well that she had to do everything in her power to put her dreadful mistake behind her and ensure that he never knew what she'd done. It would crush him. Oh, sure, he wouldn't show it. He'd carry on working and being the incredible man he was. But now she understood that on the inside he'd be bleeding as if he'd swallowed razor blades.

A timer went off in the kitchen, and she rose to her feet.

"Dinner's ready," she managed to say without any trace of the turmoil she was feeling in her voice. "Come on up to the table."

Keaton followed her to the kitchen instead. "Can I help with anything?"

"Thanks, you can take the salad through. Oh, and bring the wine to the table. I think we're going to need it tonight, don't you?"

He smiled at her again, this time with a little more warmth behind it. "Good thinking."

They talked business during dinner, discussing how her site visit had gone today and doing more risk assessment on the upcoming stage of the project. It was only when they were clearing the table together and stacking the dishwasher that Honor began to steer their conversation back to a more personal subject.

"Keaton, I've been thinking," she started.

"Hmm?"

"Let's set a date for the wedding. A real date. Something soon. We don't need a big fuss. We both work too hard to plan anything too elaborate. I'd be happy with a ceremony at your parents' place, in the ballroom overlooking the lake. Wouldn't you?"

"Do you mean summer next year?"

She drew in a deep breath. "If we apply for a license tomorrow, we could make it sooner than that—maybe late January or early February. We can keep the numbers down, cater finger food rather than an ostentatious sit-down meal with a bunch of people we barely know. What do you think?"

"Sounds like you've been giving it some serious thought."

He was hedging, and it made frustration ripple through her. Wasn't he keen to consolidate their relationship? Didn't he want to take their future plans to the next level at all?

"Of course I've been giving it serious thought," she retorted sharply. "We need to set a date, Keaton. We've been sitting on the fence about it for far too long."

He grimaced. "January is too soon." When she started to protest, he put up a hand. "No, hear me out. We both have far too much going on at work right now to even think about a wedding next month. Besides, it wouldn't be fair to Mom. You know how much she enjoys planning things in advance. For her the anticipation is everything."

Honor felt his words like a blow. His mother's happiness was more important than hers? She scratched the thought from her mind even as it formed. Nancy was a warm and loving woman who had welcomed Honor into their family without as much as a second thought. It was churlish to think he was putting Nancy before her, even if it did feel like that.

"Don't you want to be married?" she couldn't help asking.

"Yes, *I do*." He grinned at the words. "See, I'm even practicing for the big day."

She couldn't help but give him a smile in return. Not often, but sometimes, he could be a total goof, and that tugged at her heart so hard. But even so, there was still no sign of his committing to a date for their wedding.

Keaton continued, "Look, why don't we sleep on it?"

He stepped up close, put his arms around her and bent to kiss her. But at the last minute, Honor turned her face away. To soften the rejection, she nuzzled into the side of his neck. She couldn't help it. She didn't want half-hearted from him anymore. She wanted it all. She wanted heart-stopping love. She wanted breath-taking passion. If they kissed now, she knew they would both be merely going through the motions. And if they made love? Well, she couldn't even allow her thoughts to go there. Not with the memory of Logan imprinted on her mind. She was every kind of awful bitch and she deserved all kinds of hell for this. But right now, she couldn't do it.

Honor pulled free of him.

"It's late," she said with genuine regret in her voice.

"You want me to go?" Keaton sounded surprised.

"I'm sorry. I'm tired, and I think that tonight I'd prefer to be alone."

Keaton's lips firmed into a straight line. It was about the only way he ever expressed displeasure or irritation.

"I don't think I'll ever understand you, Honor. One minute you're pressing for a wedding date and the next you're literally pushing me away? Is this some payback because I wouldn't agree to getting married next month?"

"No! Of course not. I'm sorry. I shouldn't have pushed you on that. I know you're dealing with a lot right now. But I am tired. I'll see you in the office tomorrow, okay?"

"Yeah, sure."

Keaton turned, but she could see he was annoyed with her. She'd be annoyed, too, if he'd done the same thing.

"Keaton?" she called as he walked toward the front door.

He stopped and turned.

"Yes?"

Suddenly she felt unbearably vulnerable. She'd crossed a line last night, and there might never be any turning back. Maybe she should have slept with Keaton tonight, but for some reason she felt as if that would be an even larger insult to him than turning him down.

"We're going to be okay, aren't we?"

His eyes met hers, and she caught her breath in the growing silence between them.

"Sure."

And then he was gone.

Five

She barely slept, and when she went into work early the next morning, Honor was irritated to find there was someone already in her office. In fact, the unwelcome guest was sitting at a desk that hadn't been there yesterday and her couches had been moved out. She frowned as she entered then felt her stomach plummet to her feet as she recognized Logan Parker.

How did she know so instantly it was him, she wondered, when only the day before yesterday she'd thought he was Keaton? Was it the way he held his head, the set of his shoulders? On first glance, he could have been his twin, but Honor knew on a far more primal level that this was not her fiancé.

"What are you doing in my office?" she asked as she stepped through the doorway.

He lifted his head and met her furious gaze. "Our office," he said calmly, then turned his attention back to his computer screen.

"You can't be serious," she seethed.

"Look, it wasn't my choice. Apparently the office Douglas wanted me to use is undergoing a refit, so this won't be forever."

"And he couldn't find you anywhere else?"

Logan gestured to the open plan area beyond her fishbowl of an office. Every available space was taken up by her design team.

"Take it up with the boss if you have an issue."

"I most definitely will," she huffed as she slung her coat on the stand in the corner of the room and went to her desk.

She sat down and booted up her computer, but she couldn't help but be vitally aware of the man sitting just across from her. In the end she gave up any pretense of trying to work.

"Care to tell me exactly why you're here?"

Logan closed his laptop screen and looked up at her. "Douglas spent a lot of time explaining the company structure to me yesterday. He's intrigued by what I do in New Zealand and wants me to consult on possibly incorporating some of my firm's ideas into Richmond Developments. As you're the head of the design team, he felt we would have a lot to discuss."

"And you didn't tell him anything?"

"Anything? What's to tell? I hardly know you or what you do."

He looked at her then, his light gray eyes boring

into hers. She shivered, but the reaction had nothing to do with the temperature in the office and everything to do with the vivid memory of those very same eyes pinned on her as he'd entered her body.

"Exactly," she said, feeling more flustered than she cared to admit.

"You and Keaton have a nice dinner last night?"

He asked the question casually, but she saw the muscle working at the side of his jaw. He definitely wasn't as casual about this as he was projecting, she thought with a sting of satisfaction.

"We had a truly wonderful evening together," she lied. Not for a moment was she going to admit that the evening had been awkward and discouraging. "And you? Was dinner with Douglas and Nancy what you hoped for?"

"Hoped for?" He quirked a brow.

"The return of the long-lost son. You know."

She almost instantly regretted her words. None of this was his fault, and yet she seemed bound and determined to paint him as the villain in the situation.

"It was a nice evening," he replied noncommittally. "They have a lovely home."

"It's where Keaton and Kristin grew up. Must have felt strange being there and knowing you were left out of that," she said, more softly this time.

"Yeah, but I wasn't exactly deprived in my childhood. I had a roof over my head and the love of my extended family. My mother and my grandparents gave me everything they thought I needed."

An awkward silence fell between them for a moment. Honor felt compelled to break it.

"So, what exactly are you working on?"

"Douglas gave me the specs of the block of buildings Richmond Developments bought last month."

"The waterfront block?"

"Yeah."

This was like squeezing blood out of a stone. "And?"

"I'm studying the plans, the layout of the land, historical engineering reports."

"He already has plans drawn for that project. Why is he getting you to look at it?"

"He's open to repurposing the existing structure versus demolition and a new build."

"You do know that the demo team is already booked for later this month."

"Which obviously doesn't give me a lot of time for a counterproposal."

He gave her a pointed look, as if to say, *kindly shut up and let me get on with it.* She felt the hot sting of a blush suffuse her cheeks.

"Don't you think that might end up being a waste of time?"

He shrugged, and the movement was oddly sexy. "Maybe, maybe not. I've got no stake in this, so I have nothing to lose. But I do think that Douglas might be surprised at how potentially lucrative this could be for the company."

Logan made a decision. He was sick of this dancing around the very large elephant in the room, and Honor's passive-aggressive demeanor was really ticking him off. He wasn't the bad guy here, and it was about time she accepted that.

"That's a pretty big diamond you're wearing on your finger," he said, gesturing toward her left hand.

She paled visibly, and he saw her start to worry at her ring with the thumb of her left hand.

"Care to explain where that was two nights ago?"

Twin spots of high color appeared on her wan cheeks.

"I, uh…when I got back to my room, I took it off," she eventually admitted.

"I'm guessing you thought I was him," he said.

Logan's voice was flat and devoid of emotion, but inside his guts were churning. Knowing he'd slept with his brother's fiancée made him feel ill and had plagued him from the minute he'd been formally introduced to her yesterday. Keaton hadn't exactly been the most welcoming, and the last thing he wanted to do was give his brother any further reasons to hate him.

"I did. We, um, things have been a bit…" Her voice trailed off for a moment. "We've both been very busy with work. To be totally honest with you, we, um, hadn't been together in a while, and I thought he'd come to the hotel to surprise me and to inject a bit of fun back into our relationship."

Logan stood there, not saying a word, just watching her as she squirmed beneath his gaze. He'd spent much of yesterday furiously angry. Not that he'd shown it, but he'd alternately been irate at her then equally incensed with himself. Before that night, he'd never indulged in a one-night stand, ever. If he'd simply handed her key in to reception, as he ought to have done, none of this would have happened and he wouldn't be here, in their shared office, his senses tormented by the scent of her and his body plagued by the memory of what it felt like to make love to her. But if she hadn't approached him in the first place…?

How could she not have told the difference between them?

"Together? As in intimate together?" he probed.

She nodded.

"And you didn't think my accent odd?"

"To be honest, until you were in my room I barely listened to a word you said, and even after that I didn't stop to think beyond the fact that you were probably just in character, as it were."

"In character?" He shook his head. "So what now?"

"What do you mean, what now?"

"What happens next? Are you going to tell him?"

He saw the muscles in the slender column of her throat work as she swallowed hard.

"I… I don't know. I honestly thought you were him. In my own mind, I was having sex with my fiancé, not some random stranger in a bar. Believe me when I say I never do that kind of thing."

"Nor I," Logan admitted before sinking back into his chair. "So where to, from here? Do we just pretend it never happened?"

"That would be my preference," she said in a stilted voice.

He looked at her and couldn't help but remember how silky soft her skin was, or how responsive she'd been to his touch. He was getting hard just thinking about it, which was a really stupid thing to do. Thinking was dangerous, and touching her again—hell, that would be hazardous on a whole different level. He wondered how the hell he was going to stand being cooped up in the same office with her during work hours, and, no doubt, have to continue seeing her with his brother.

It was no less punishment than he deserved.

"Okay, so we never met before yesterday morning in Douglas's office."

Her features brightened with hope. "You can do that? Forget we—"

"I can. I have to. We both have to. I don't think you quite understand what I have at risk here. When I discovered who I was my sense of self was completely yanked out from under me. Have you got any idea what that was like?"

She looked at him, her eyes never leaving his face for a second. He saw the compassion there. But he didn't want compassion from Honor Gould. No, he wanted everything he couldn't have with her, but if he could begin anew with some form of understanding between them, then maybe they could get through this.

He continued. "She'd kept all the newspaper clippings about my abduction. Can you imagine that? Now that I've uncovered the truth about who I am, I don't want to destroy my only chance with the family I've just discovered. So, in answer to your question, yes, I can do that. I can forget, or at least pretend to, that our night together ever happened."

"I'm so sorry, Logan." She shook her head and lowered her gaze, but not before he saw the abject shame that filled her eyes. "I've honestly only been thinking about what this whole awful situation means to me. I never stopped to think how it impacted you as well."

"Then we're agreed?"

She got up from her chair and walked over to him. "Yes, we are. Care to shake on it?"

He accepted the hand she offered but was unprepared for the instant physical awareness that tingled through him at her touch. This was going to be so much harder than anything he'd ever done before. But he had to succeed, because if he didn't, he stood to lose everything he'd ever wanted his whole life. He let go of her hand quickly, before he could do something stupid like tug her forward into his arms and kiss her again like his body was urging him to do.

Douglas Richmond breezed into their office, and Logan fought to keep his expression calm when, right now, he felt like a kid caught with his hand in the cookie jar. He glanced at Honor, who looked similarly afflicted, and they moved apart as if they'd been caught doing so much more than innocently shaking hands.

"Ah, good to see the two of you getting along. Sorry I didn't get to discuss the new office setup with you before you got in this morning, Honor. But since I want the two of you to work closely together, it made sense. Any objections?" Douglas stared at her as if challenging her to argue.

To Logan's surprise, she held her own.

"Actually, I would have preferred notice, but I'm

prepared to accommodate Mr. Parker for as long as he's here."

Douglas laughed. "As long as he's here? We've waited thirty-four years for our family to be complete. If Logan's claim is validated, the last thing Nancy and I would want is for him to go racing back to the far reaches of the Southern Hemisphere again. I hope I can rely on you to make him feel welcome, Honor. You know how important family is to us."

Logan observed how she stiffened. This was likely her worst nightmare. Not only having to face up to her mistake, but having to work closely with him every day would put them both under a great deal of strain.

And temptation.

"Of course you can rely on me, Douglas. You know that. I'd do anything for this family."

"*Our* family," Douglas corrected gently. "You're a part of us, too, Honor. Logan has some very exciting ideas for Richmond Developments going forward. I want you to include him in your day-to-day activities so he can get a feel for how we operate. And, now, I suggest that the two of you come with me to the waterfront site so Logan can take a look at the buildings and layout there."

Logan nodded. "If you don't mind, I'd like to stop by my hotel room and get my camera so I can get some high-resolution images."

"Of course. Honor? You're free?"

Logan had the distinct impression that even if she wasn't, Douglas expected her to drop everything and join them.

"Let me check my calendar," she said and went through the motions of checking on her computer before nodding. "I can make myself available now, but I need to be back here by midday for another meeting."

"Good, good," Douglas said, clasping his hands and rubbing his palms together. "I'll meet you down in the parking garage in ten."

And without waiting another moment, he was gone.

Logan turned to Honor. "Is he always like that?"

"Always expecting everyone to fall in line? Yeah, pretty much."

"It's an imposition having me in here, isn't it?"

"It's not my place to say. I'm merely on the staff here."

"But you're engaged to my brother," he couldn't help adding. "Douglas said you're family."

"Yes, I am. And I'd be grateful if you'd continue to be mindful of that. I know you don't want to lose your new family, but I, too, have a lot at stake here."

"Noted," Logan said abruptly.

They left the office together and headed for the elevators. On the ride down, Honor looked as though she was mulling something over. After a few seconds, she spat it out.

"Did Douglas talk to Keaton about this new direction for Richmond Developments?"

"Not last night. As you'll recall, you two had a prior engagement. So, too, did Kristin."

Honor shifted a little on her feet. "Don't you think he should be apprised of this new development? After all, he is the vice president of the company. You might be the bright, shiny new toy for Douglas and Nancy, but Keaton's been here doing the heavy lifting since he graduated from college."

"I came to Seattle with a business idea and the hope that I could find acceptance within a family I had the right to know all my life but was cheated of." Logan defended himself, surprised by her sudden onslaught. "I'm not here to step on anybody's toes."

"It may pay to remind Douglas of that. He tends to get an idea in his head and run with it, at the expense of everything and everyone else."

"Thanks for the heads-up. I'll raise it with him as soon as I get the opportunity."

The elevator doors slid open and they walked out together, their footsteps synchronized as if they did this every day. Was Honor this in tune with his brother, Logan wondered before slamming the door on that line of thought.

"We wait here," she directed him when she came to a halt. "The limousine will be here shortly."

"Limousine? Douglas doesn't drive?"

"Douglas doesn't do anything himself that he can pay someone else to do for him," she said.

"I've always preferred to do things myself where I can. I find it keeps me sharper."

She looked at him with a surprised expression. "We have that in common."

"I suspect we have a great deal more than that in common," he commented.

And just like that, the heat level between them rose dangerously.

Six

"Don't. Just don't go there," she admonished. The elevator doors pinged open behind them just as a long black vehicle drove into the underground parking lot. "Ah, here's the car and here's Douglas, right on cue."

Logan had the distinct impression she was about to add the words *thank goodness*. He stepped forward and opened the door for Honor and his father and slid onto the wide bench seat next to her after they'd settled in the car. Honor shifted just a little farther away from him, making her point perfectly clear. Douglas, thankfully, appeared to be oblivious.

After stopping briefly at Logan's hotel so he could retrieve his camera, they drove about half an hour to an old waterfront development surrounded by a combination of low-rise business and apartment blocks.

Logan alighted from the car and began taking random shots of the surroundings before focusing on the actual development site. Caged by temporary fencing, the collection of brick buildings looked derelict and unloved, but he could already see the warmth in the bricks and the shapes of the window openings that with new frames and glass would be like windows into the buildings' souls.

Oblivious to Honor and Douglas, he began to walk around the site, taking hundreds of photos. When he paused a moment, he saw his father watching him with a smile on his face.

"You're passionate about your work, aren't you, Logan? I can see it on your face and how you lose yourself in what you're doing."

Logan nodded. "Places like this need to be preserved wherever possible—that's what I'm passionate about. Finding the most cost-effective way to hold on to the past, while making sure the buildings can withstand the demands of the future in the most ecologically friendly way, is the challenge. Tell me more about the site. When was it built, and what was its main purpose?"

Douglas went into a detailed history about how the site had primarily consisted of warehouses for the past century and a half. Logan found himself nodding and making mental notes as they walked through the ground floor of one of the buildings. His hands itched to make drawings and concept designs. First, he'd do it all on paper, old-school. Then he'd load the necessary specs into his computer and use his design software. Obviously the architectural design team back at the office would need to consult on his suggestions, to make sure everything fit in with all planning requirements, but his mind was spinning in a million different directions with an expanding dream for the space. And if he could present his dream to Douglas and see him take Richmond Developments on a new trajectory, well, that would make everything all the sweeter.

He knew he'd taken a big risk in coming here, both from a professional and personal point of view, but when he'd looked at the big picture, he'd known that finding his birth family was more important than anything he'd ever done. Back home, he had an incredible team of managers and staff running his company. He was in the position where he could have as little or as much input as he wanted, which had made this the perfect time to step away and pursue his new goal of discovering his blood kin.

As they spent some time in each of the buildings, Logan sensed Honor's impatience to return to the office. He could have spent the entire day here; in fact, he probably would sometime in the next week or so, but for now he needed to ensure he stayed on the right side of Honor Gould.

"I think I have everything I need for now. Thanks for taking the time out of your day, both of you, and for bringing me out here," Logan said as he put his camera back in its case and slung the strap over his shoulder.

"It's interesting watching you work," Douglas commented as they walked back to the car. "You approach everything with an artist's eye, I think, rather than from a practical point of view."

"I like to think I come at it from both angles, but I guess you're right. If you can't see the beauty in a thing before you start, why would you continue with it?"

Douglas barked a laugh. "A bit like when you meet the woman of your dreams, right?"

Logan's mouth twisted into a smile. "Something like that. Say, Honor, were you already working up color palettes for the new buildings Richmond Developments had planned to build here?"

"Of course. I've had a team on this project full-time for a month. The apartment specs were established even before that."

She sounded ticked off. As if her team's hard work may all have been for nothing.

"I'd like to see them if you're free this afternoon."

"I'm not."

The sharpness of her tone earned her an odd look from her future father-in-law.

"Perhaps tomorrow morning, then," Logan suggested.

"I'll have my assistant show you the concepts when we get back to the office."

Ah, so she was going to be like that. He'd obviously encroached on her work territory and maybe she also needed to reduce her contact with him. He watched her as she walked toward the limousine, ahead of him and Douglas. She ducked into the back of the car, and he saw she'd chosen the seat with her back to the driver.

"She's a fine-looking woman, Honor," Douglas

commented as they neared the car. "But sometimes I think she and Keaton are too similar for theirs to be a truly happy marriage."

Logan was surprised at his father's observation. "How so?"

"They're each so intent on climbing the corporate ladder at Richmond Developments, I think they've forgotten to take time to let their relationship grow. I feel like they're still stuck in that dating phase and that they haven't moved past it. Nancy keeps telling me not to worry, but I can't help feeling those two are just going through the motions. Life, happiness—they're worth more than that."

Logan didn't know how to respond, but he didn't have to as Douglas was now occupied with climbing into the car. He took the seat Honor had occupied on the way to the site, while Logan now sat directly opposite Honor. He could see from the moment their knees brushed—the barest touch, but one he perversely engineered before he slid back farther into his seat—that she regretted being forced to stare at him, or past him, for the duration of the journey back to the office.

Honor couldn't wait to get to her meeting and away from the all-too-tempting presence of Logan Parker. Honestly, watching him at the project site should have been an exercise in complete and utter boredom. Instead, she found herself studying the expression on his face as he eyed the buildings and took photos and wondering what on earth was going through his mind. Sometimes his thoughts were as clear as glass, as excitement lit his pale gray eyes and animated his expression. Other times he was more pensive. And then there were the times he'd looked at her—whether by accident or design.

Each time their gazes had locked, she'd felt it like a physical touch and her body had responded in kind. Now, back at the office, she couldn't wait to put some distance between them. He was altogether too unnerving—and, she reminded herself, he was not Keaton.

She'd been unable to sleep last night after Keaton had left, tied up in knots at refusing him, yet at the same time still craving his twin in ways that shocked her. She'd never thought herself to be particularly motivated by sex, but after the night at the hotel... *No!* She had to put that out of her mind. What she'd done was reprehensible and, deep down, she knew she couldn't be intimate with Keaton while this awful secret stood between them.

Logan had agreed to keep things quiet, but could she trust him with what was inarguably the biggest and most destructive secret of her entire life? This went way past the occasional childhood shoplifting at the grocery store when her mom hadn't had enough money to buy a loaf of bread or a carton of milk. And, besides, she'd always suspected the store owner had turned a blind eye when hunger had forced her to steal. A compassionate man, he'd known that her mom was oftentimes incapable of looking after her daughter.

Honor blinked and had to drag her thoughts back to the present when she realized Douglas was talking to her as they entered the elevator from the parking garage at Richmond Tower.

"I'm sorry, my mind was already at my next meeting," she lied.

"That's what I like about you, Honor. Always thinking ahead," Douglas said with a smug smile. "What I was saying is that you need to include Logan in your meeting. It's with the new eco–wall covering company, isn't it?"

"It is, but I was going to get Steve to go through color palettes with Logan this afternoon."

Douglas made a dismissive gesture with his hand. "Logan has more important things to do than study color palettes. I want him up to speed with everything as quickly as possible, and the only way to do that is to be on the ground with eyes and ears open."

Honor gritted her teeth. "Logan did request to see the color concepts this afternoon," she reminded Douglas.

"Yes, I did and, to be honest, I'm still a bit slammed with jet lag so I'd appreciate the opportunity to spend some time in the office and keep absorbing ideas for the new project. I can spend all day tomorrow with Honor instead."

All day tomorrow? She shuddered at the thought. It was going to be impossible for her to get through her work with him shadowing her every move and thought.

"Fine," she said in a tone that left no one in any doubt that it was anything but. "Now, if you gentlemen will excuse me, I have a meeting to get to."

She left the two of them behind her as she made a

sharp turn and headed to the conference room she'd booked for the afternoon. She was so annoyed and distracted that she was almost at the door before she realized she'd left her notes and her computer behind in her office. No, she corrected herself, not her office anymore—hers and Logan's. Honor's hands clenched into tight fists at her sides as she did an about-face and strode swiftly to retrieve the materials she needed. When she got there, she didn't immediately see Logan until she was almost on top of him, and they both moved to the same side in a failed attempt to avoid a full-on crash.

She flung up her hands as their bodies connected, her palms pressed hard against the firmness of his chest. Instant awareness coursed through her as she remembered what it had felt like to touch him, skin to skin. Logan caught her upper arms to steady her and she instantly took a step back, breaking the unwanted contact as quickly as she could.

"I'm sorry," she said a little too breathlessly. "I wasn't looking where I was going."

"It's okay. Steve mentioned you'd need these for your meeting, so I was bringing them along for you."

"Thank you," she said stiffly, taking her laptop case from him. She quickly checked that all the papers were tucked in with her laptop, which of course they were, because Steve was nothing if not efficient. "Right, well, this will take me the balance of the day, so I'll see you tomorrow."

Without waiting for him to respond, she turned on her heel and stalked away. Damn him for being here.

Damn him for even existing, she thought fiercely. Despite all her best intentions, she appeared to be incapable of being in the same space as Logan Parker without her entire body going up in metaphorical flames. What the heck was wrong with her? She had a fiancé already. A man who in every way resembled the one she was walking away from as if her life depended on it.

Every way? a little voice asked at the back of her mind.

Her stomach tightened into a knot as she forced herself to acknowledge the point of difference in the two men. Yes, she loved Keaton and she had promised to marry him. He was handsome and clever and, on occasion, showed wit that hugely appealed to her. But he didn't set her on fire the way Logan Parker did. Why not?

Honor fussed with her engagement ring all the way to the meeting room, and even when she got there she struggled to get her thoughts under control. It wasn't until her supplier and their team arrived for the meeting that she managed to switch off the clamor in her mind and focus on what she needed to do. One day she and Keaton would run Richmond Developments together as husband and wife. As Douglas and Nancy did now. They were of a like mind. They had the same dreams and visions for their joint future. This was the road to ensure lifetime security. She needed to remember that.

Logan was working on his laptop when Kristin came to the door of the office.

"Oh, you're here," she said. "I was looking for Honor."

"She's tied up in a supplier meeting all afternoon. Do you want to leave her a message?"

"No, I'll get hold of her later." Kristin made no pretense of hiding her nosiness as she tried to see what he had up on his screen. "Aren't those pictures of the new development site?" she asked.

"Yeah, we went there today. I'm working on a plan to persuade your father to save most of the buildings."

"Seriously? You know we don't do that kind of thing here. It's not cost-effective."

Logan shrugged. "Well, we'll see."

"Trust me, I know about these things. I don't run the finance department just for fun. There's no way you can recover the costs of repurposing those buildings as quickly as we would with a new build, if at all."

She walked all the way into the office and stood there, arms crossed, feet planted shoulder width apart and looking as combative as she'd been yesterday.

"Sometimes it's not just about making money," Logan commented.

She laughed. "Are you sure you're related to us?"

He couldn't help it. He laughed out loud. "Yeah, I'm sure. Hey, do you know if the DNA results are back yet?"

"I don't think even Dad's money can rush those kinds of results. I'm pretty sure it'll be another few days, but even so, he's starting to sound like he doesn't need the proof."

"Do you?"

She uncrossed her arms and sank into the chair opposite his desk. "You look like my brother, but you don't sound like him."

"And yet, I know, in here—" he tapped his chest "—I'm your brother. How's that for weird?"

She frowned a little before responding. "So what happens if you are who you think you are? Are you staying here in Seattle? Forging a role for yourself at Richmond Developments?"

"It's still fluid for now," Logan admitted. "I have a strong team running my business back home, but there's always a need for a hand at the tiller. It was my brainchild, after all, and I'd hate to see anything change or slip while I was here."

"Ever considered a career in politics? That's a non-answer if ever I heard one."

He cracked a half smile. "True. I owe you better than that if we're siblings, don't I?" He sighed and leaned back in his chair. "To be honest, I'd like to think I could forge a place here as long as I don't step on any toes. I know you and Keaton have both worked in the family firm since you left college and probably even before that."

Kristin nodded. "And?"

"And I don't want to be that newcomer who walks all over you to get what he wants. That said, I should have been a part of this family and Richmond Developments all along. I want my place in *my* family."

Kristin nodded again. "I get that. But until the test results come back, you're in limbo, aren't you? What's the arrangement back in New Zealand? Are you on leave for a set period or have you appointed an interim CEO in your absence?"

"At this stage, I'm on leave for three months."

Kristin tipped her head to one side and looked at him seriously. "This is really important to you, isn't it? It's not just a matter of finding your birth family. It's more a matter of finding your entire identity."

Logan felt some of the tension he hadn't even realized he was holding in his body ease just a little. "That's exactly it. I had to give it my best shot. I figured that within three months I could prove my link to this family and discover whether or not I fit here. If I don't, well, I will always have my other family and my work back in New Zealand. I don't plan to abandon either."

Kristin nodded slightly, then her expression became curious. "Just how are your family back home handling your trip here?"

Logan twirled a pen in his fingers as he considered his answer. "Some of them are worried about what this will bring down on my late mother's name, especially with her having abducted me. But most of my cousins understand why this is so important to me. I'm not turning my back on them. I will always love and respect them. My grandmother is still living, and she gave me her blessing. We still consider each other family. End of story."

"We don't have any living grandparents," Kristin said bluntly. "They died before I was born, and Keaton was too small to remember them. Do you think your grandmother would accept us, too?"

Logan grinned widely. "She'd welcome you with

open arms. If you're connected to me, you're absolutely connected to her, too. As well as all my cousins and, trust me, there are a lot of them."

"Mom and Dad were both only children, so we don't have cousins here. I think I'd like to be part of a larger extended family."

"Looks like we both stand to benefit if the results come back positive," Logan said.

Watching the expression on Kristin's face soften as they talked about his background gave him an insight into his sister that he wasn't expecting. She was a powerhouse here at Richmond Developments, but inside she was still a person who cherished family ties. She was looking for a place to belong, just as he was. He began to feel a glimmer of hope that she was on the path to accepting him and his place within the family.

"Those are great shots. What type of camera did you use? It wasn't your phone camera, was it?" Kristin asked, abruptly changing the subject as she turned to look at his computer screen. Clearly the time for family communion was over.

"No." He reached down beside the desk, took his camera from its case and handed it over to her. "I use this when I'm on a job, but I usually have it with me when I'm out and about, too. I don't want to miss anything that could be a source of inspiration."

Kristin lit up when she saw the camera, and he was intrigued to find they had a love of photography in common.

"Oh hell," Kristin said after a few more minutes of

discussion. "I'm supposed to be elsewhere. We'll need to continue this later."

Logan stood as she did and held out his hand. Kristin hesitated a moment before taking it.

"Thank you," he said.

"For what?"

"For talking to me like I'm not the enemy. I'm not, you know."

She gave a short nod. "Yeah, well, I'm not the one you have to convince."

Seven

It became eminently clear at a dinner at his parents' house the following Sunday just whom he did need to convince—Keaton. His twin was as distrustful as he'd been on day one, and there was absolutely no sign of any acceptance or friendship coming from his direction. In fact, he appeared more openly hostile than before.

Honor, too, had become even more standoffish. But he knew she was aware of exactly where he was throughout the course of the entire evening, and he knew that because he was equally, painfully aware of her. Neither Honor nor Keaton had said more than a word or two to him all evening, nor to each other, to be honest. But it looked as though that was going to change any moment now, Logan realized, as he watched his brother stride toward him with a look of determination painted clearly on his face.

"Keaton, good to see you. Our paths haven't exactly crossed the past few days, and I'd like to catch up when you're free," Logan said as an opening gambit. He certainly wasn't expecting what came next.

"Stay away from my fiancée," Keaton said in a low voice.

"I beg your pardon?"

"I said, stay away from Honor. I've seen the way you look at her, and she doesn't need the pressure of having to ward off unwanted attention. Be a gentleman, Parker. Hands off."

Logan squared his shoulders and stared his brother down.

"Hands off? That would imply I'm trying to be hands on."

Had someone mentioned seeing the two of them at the hotel the other night? Was everything about to blow up in Logan's face? Surely his parents wouldn't be so welcoming if they knew what he and Honor had done. His gaze flicked past Keaton's shoulder to where Honor sat chatting with Kristin.

"Even now you can't stop looking at her. It's making both of us uncomfortable. Stop it," Keaton said firmly.

"I'm sorry," Logan began, deciding to take a placatory line rather than engaging in the full-on confrontation his alpha side wanted.

Keaton was right. He had been unable to keep his gaze off Honor tonight. She looked, as always, stunningly beautiful, but there was an air of fragility about her that hadn't been there the night he'd met her. It called on every one of his instincts to protect her and make her world right so the confident woman he'd met could come forth again. But it wasn't his place to offer her that protection, and he kept having to remind himself of that.

"She's a beautiful and clever woman, Keaton, and I'm sorry if I've made either of you uncomfortable," Logan continued. "Unfortunately, your father has put us in her office together. I can ask to be moved, if that would make you, and Honor, more at ease."

"Look, I can accept that Dad, for whatever idiotic reason that's currently taken his normally rational mind hostage, thinks that the two of you need to work together. Just keep it business, okay? Even now you're staring at her as if she's a triple-decker burger and you haven't eaten for a week."

"Triple-decker burger?" Logan couldn't help it—he burst out laughing.

Keaton had the grace to grin back at him. "What can I say? I'm hungry. Mom's idea of dinner is not really suited to people with a genuine appetite."

"Want to head out for a triple decker once this is over? It would give us a chance to talk, just the two of us."

Logan knew that if an olive branch was to be extended, it had to come from him. He was the outsider here and if he wasn't prepared to do what was necessary to make his brother happy, then he didn't deserve to be here, either. But should his brother's happiness come at his own expense? He clamped down on the thought before it could bloom into anything else.

Keaton was shaking his head. "Sorry, I have an early start in the morning. Business meeting in San Antonio, then on to Houston and up to Dallas over the next few days, so I'm heading home soon."

"Maybe another time, then."

"Sure. When I get back. We'll sort something out."

Keaton started to turn away, but Logan stopped him.

"Keaton?"

"Yeah?"

"Don't worry about me with Honor. I respect the fact that she's your fiancée, and I won't do anything to upset her."

Keaton stared at him hard, as if to gauge whether he was telling the truth, and for a moment it was unsettling looking so directly into a living mirror of himself. Whatever Keaton saw reflected back in Logan's eyes must have satisfied him, because he nodded and offered his brother his hand. The two men shook and then Keaton went to make his apologies to his parents before leaving. Honor, too, made her excuses and joined him.

As Logan watched them leave, he couldn't help but wonder if he'd end up being proved a liar. His desire for Honor had not abated. Not when she'd sniped at him in the office. Not when she'd all but ignored him on a site visit. Not when she'd studiously avoided him at this family dinner. Was her bad temper because she continued to fight her own attraction for him, or was it that he made her uncomfortable like his brother had said?

Whatever it was, the knowledge that Honor was with Keaton should have been enough to quell any feelings he had for her. The very thought of his brother's hands on her was enough to send a murderous rage through his mind the likes of which he'd never experienced before. And that, in itself, was more than enough warning that he needed to get some level of control on his feelings. No, better than control. He needed to rid himself of them altogether.

Honor Gould was strictly out of bounds.

As Keaton drove her home, Honor mulled over the fact that he was going to be away for several days. While he was around, she could tell herself that the magnetic pull she felt from Logan Parker was nothing to worry about. But with him gone? She gave herself a hard mental shake as they pulled into the parking garage at her apartment building. She was made of sterner stuff than her mother. She was far more driven to succeed and far more motivated. She was not going to let Logan Parker derail her lifelong dream. She hadn't worked this hard for this long to see it go by the wayside all because of some crazy hormonal reaction to a man who looked exactly like the one she'd promised to spend the rest of her life with.

And she and Keaton would have a great life together. She had no doubt of that. They were on the same page with everything from how many children they wanted to how they planned to continue to work together. Okay, so they were a little lacking in the passion stakes—she could live with that.

But could he?

She'd never truly asked herself that question before today. Was she forcing him to settle for less than he deserved? Was he happy looking forward to a tepid love life for the next fifty or sixty years? She hated that she was second-guessing herself all of a sudden and that she was second-guessing Keaton, too. It was patently evident that they needed to talk. She had to be certain he was happy. She did love him and she wanted happiness for him, and more. But was she the right person to give that to him?

"Are you coming up?" she asked as he pulled into one of the two parking spaces allocated to her apartment.

"I'll see you to your door, the way I always do," he said with a smile.

"I was hoping that maybe we could do a bit more than that."

"More than that?"

"Yes, like talk about our future."

He sighed a little. "Let's go upstairs."

He got out of the car, walked around to her door and opened it for her. Always the consummate gentleman. She loved that about him, she truly did, but manners didn't make a relationship, did they? They both needed more than that.

Upstairs in her apartment, Honor offered him coffee.

"No, thanks. What did you want to talk about, specifically?" he asked, not even taking a seat.

Honor drew in a deep breath. This would be so much

easier if he'd just sit down instead of looking like he was ready to bolt for the door at the earliest opportunity.

"Us. I feel like there's a distance between us lately, and it's growing. Are you happy, Keaton?" she asked him, studying his expression carefully.

She'd always been able to tell if he was being truthful, but right now his eyes were shuttered and the set of his face made him look more distant than she'd ever seen him.

"There's a lot going on, not to mention I have to leave on the red eye for San Antonio in a few hours. Look, can't this wait until I get back?" he hedged.

Honor took a step toward him. "This is important, Keaton. I need to know. Are you happy?"

He closed his eyes briefly before looking straight back into hers, and in that moment Honor regretted pushing the issue and dreaded what she was about to hear.

"I think we should consider taking a break," he said, bluntly.

"A break away together?" she asked hopefully, even though she knew that wasn't what he meant.

"No, apart."

Honor made a small strangled sound. Suddenly, it felt as though everything she'd ever worked for and wanted was slipping out of her grasp.

"Look, I know this probably comes as a shock, but I feel like lately we're on different wavelengths. I've tried to ignore it. Even tried to blame it on the resurrection of my sainted, long-lost brother. But if I'm totally honest with myself, this sense of separation started before his arrival on the scene. You've felt it, too, haven't you?"

Honor found herself nodding. She knew exactly what he was talking about, even if she hadn't wanted to admit it.

Keaton took a step toward her and wrapped her in his arms. "Look, let's take some time to think about what we really want."

"I thought we knew what we wanted," she said, her voice breaking on the last few words.

He sighed and shook his head slightly. "So did I. Look, I'm gone most of this week. Let's use the time apart to figure things out, and if we need more space when I get back, we'll take however long is necessary till we can agree on our paths for the future."

Paths? Did he mean separate paths? Honor couldn't bring herself to verbalize the question, because she was afraid of what he might say.

"Okay?" he prompted.

"It'll have to be okay, won't it?" she said carefully. "When we marry, it's going to be forever. Like you say, we need to be sure."

"I'm sorry, Honor. With everything going on with work and the family, this is just one more log on the fire, isn't it?"

"As a couple we should be supporting one another through this. I'm not certain that taking time out is the best idea."

She had to fight for this, for him, even if it felt as though she was a drowning woman grasping at straws.

"Trust me, Honor. Even if you don't need the space

to think, I do. Everything that I took as a given in my life has been turned upside down with Logan's arrival. It's making me take a good long look at everything that's important to me, and I'm coming to realize that some of those things aren't as important as I thought."

"And I'm one of those things?" Sudden burning tears filled her eyes and began to track down her cheeks.

He made a sound of frustration and lifted his hand to wipe away her tears.

"Our relationship is important. I love you, Honor. Truly, I do, but do I love you enough to marry you and spend the rest of our lives together? I'm not sure about that anymore."

The fact that he was verbalizing what she'd been feeling herself was no balm to her panicked mind. She pulled free of his arms and he stepped back immediately, as if grateful for the space. Fighting to hold on to her sanity, Honor forced a teary smile to her face.

"You'd better go. You have an early start, as you said."

"Are you going to be okay?"

She straightened her shoulders. "Sure."

He kissed her then, but it was not the kind of kiss lovers shared. Instead it felt more like a bittersweet expression of a regretful goodbye, and with that realization Honor knew the writing was on the wall. She walked him to the door of her apartment, twisting her engagement ring off her finger as she did so.

"Do you want this back while we're on this break?" she said, holding out her hand with the ring in her palm.

"No, of course not! And even if we—" He shook his

head firmly and took the ring from her palm and slid it back on her finger. "The ring is yours, no matter what *we* decide."

After another night with next to no sleep, Honor had worked herself into quite a state of irritation by the time she arrived in the office. As usual, Logan Parker was already settled at the desk opposite hers. Did the man never rest? He was always first in and last home. Or maybe he was just trying to impress Douglas. No, she was being churlish. He didn't have to impress Douglas or Nancy. He wasn't after the family's money. He was a millionaire in his own right; she knew that because she'd done more research on him than any uninterested person had a right to do.

Which meant what, exactly? That she *was* interested? She shoved the thought away and fought to compose herself.

"Good morning," Logan said, looking up as she set her briefcase beside her desk.

"If you say so," she answered.

"Bad night?"

Since he'd arrived on the scene, every night had been a bad night—well, almost every night—but she wasn't about to give him the pleasure of knowing that.

"I always hate it when Keaton goes away. I miss him already."

There, that was exactly what a loving fiancée should say, wasn't it? But she was such a fraud.

A rustle of movement in the hall caught her attention. She turned to see Douglas Richmond moving swiftly toward their office, and the expression on his face was one of extreme excitement.

"Glad I caught the two of you together," he said without any preamble. "I just heard that the deal fell through on a riverfront development in Portland we bid on and lost. The owners didn't want the site cleared and rebuilt on. Mentioned a whole lot of sentimental clap-trap when they turned us down, even though we offered more money. Now the buyers have backed out, saying the covenants put on the building are too restrictive. The sellers are offering it to us again if we're willing to redesign the existing structures and not do a teardown.

"I think this is a perfect opportunity for Logan to manage a project for us, and I want the two of you to head there today and do a site examination before I agree to terms. Don't let on we're too eager, but I have a feeling this could be the jewel in the crown."

"And the site we went to last week?" Logan asked.

"Figures aren't looking feasible for what you were suggesting. We can keep some of the buildings for re-tail and restaurant development, but Kristin says we need a better return on the residential side. I back her up on that. The girl knows money, and we're not just here to make friends."

Honor wondered how Logan would take the news, but if she expected him to argue with Douglas, she was disappointed. Instead, he merely shrugged.

"Got to agree with the bean counters," he said philo-sophically. "But I'm glad we can look to preserve some of the buildings at least."

Douglas nodded. "And this new project. I need you

guys on the next flight to Portland." He stated the check-in time. "Can you pack and be ready on time? My assistant has already booked you on the flight and arranged accommodation."

"I have a bag in the trunk of my car," Honor said. "I'm always ready."

"That's one of the things I always know I can rely on with you, Honor. How about you?" Douglas asked, looking at Logan.

"If we can swing past my hotel on the way to the airport, it won't take me more than ten minutes to throw some things together. It's just for one night, right?"

"Possibly two. Depends on how long it takes you to get all the information you need."

Honor hid the shudder that ran down her spine. Two days pretty much alone with Logan Parker? It was a good thing she'd had that little pep talk with herself this morning.

"We'd better get going then. I'm assuming Stella has emailed the flight details to us already?" Honor checked her email app on her phone and nodded. "Yes, they're all here."

"Good. I look forward to your report when you return. It's vitally important that this is done right. I was pretty sore when we originally lost the bid, and I don't need to tell you how much it cost us in wasted man-hours. I don't want anything to screw it up this time. Got it?"

"Got it," Logan said firmly.

Douglas nodded at them both and left as quickly as he'd arrived. Honor looked at Logan.

"Well, don't just stand there. We need to move. When the man says hurry, he means it."

"Okay, I'm moving."

Logan bent to grab his camera from the bottom drawer of his desk. The fabric of his trousers stretched tight across his butt, and the sight made something clench hard deep inside her. *Nope, nope, nope.* She forced herself to avert her gaze. She had this under control. She wasn't about to do or say anything that put her precarious future in even more jeopardy. But she couldn't resist another peek, nor could she forget what his body had felt like as it moved against hers or what his skin had felt like beneath the palms of her hands.

Palms that were growing sweaty at the thought. She couldn't stay here in this room with him right now or she might do something irreparably stupid. She walked out into the hall. Honor felt him behind her, moving quickly to catch up as she reached the elevator.

"Does everyone around here jump this fast when Douglas says so?" he drawled as he stopped next to her.

"Usually they ask how high, but then they spring into action. You don't stay here long if you don't do what he says," she said, willing the elevator to come quickly. "That's not to say he's unreasonable. He's a fair employer. But he's fiercely results-driven."

There was a ping, and the doors slid open. She and Logan stepped inside. She moved directly to the opposite wall of the car from where he stood. She knew he noticed and saw the way his jaw clenched ever so slightly. So he was irritated by her putting distance between them? She didn't care. It was the only way she could keep her equilibrium right now.

Honor tried to convince herself it was only because he looked so much like Keaton that she was drawn to him, but she knew that it was more than that. So very much more. It was attraction on a fiercely instinctive level. The kind that kept humankind alive as a species.

And it terrified her.

Eight

"What do you mean, the hotel has only one room booked for us? Obviously we require two rooms. This is unacceptable," Honor ranted at the implacable hotel receptionist.

It had been an arduous day already, and this development was the icing on a rapidly sinking cake, as far as she was concerned.

"Ma'am, we explained it to the person making the booking and they said it would be all right as you and Mr. Richmond were a couple. We are fully booked with no rooms to spare, and with several major events here in the city over the next two days, none of our other hotels have rooms available, either."

"Well, can we get a room with twin beds? Or maybe a rollaway could be brought to the room?"

She wouldn't share a bed with him. There was no way on earth she was getting that cozy with Logan again. No, if they couldn't change their room, he could find his own accommodation elsewhere.

"No, ma'am. I'm afraid not, and safety regulations do not allow for a rollaway bed in this room. Do you wish to relinquish the booking? We do have a wait list of people asking for rooms. As I said, it's a busy time."

She wanted to scream at the receptionist, but she knew the woman was simply doing her job. The trip had been planned at short notice, and clearly Stella had misunderstood exactly which Richmond brother Honor was traveling with.

"No, look, I'm sorry I was rude. I'll take the booking." She looked over her shoulder at Logan. "Can you call around and see if you can find anywhere else?"

He raised one brow. "You don't think we can share a room?"

The challenge was barely there, but it sent alarm bells ringing in her head. Did he honestly think she was going to spend the night with him in such close proximity?

"After all," Logan continued, lowering his voice, "we're both adults, aren't we? I think we can remain true to our pact. Or are you afraid that once we're behind locked doors you won't be able to control yourself?"

"Of course I can control myself," she said, stiff with disapproval.

"So you're suggesting *I* can't? That I'll be so overwhelmed by your beauty, your scent, your very nearness, that I won't be able to control myself?"

Desire spread through her like wildfire. She pushed it down, refusing to be seduced by the tone of his voice or the reaction of her wayward hormones.

"Can you guarantee you won't?" she challenged him.

"Oh yeah, I can guarantee it. I've never had to force myself on anyone, Honor, and I'm not about to start now."

She'd made him angry, and for some reason that filled her with regret.

"Let me see if I can find you somewhere else first. If there's absolutely nothing available, then we'll share."

Logan stood back and crossed his arms, observing her with an air of boredom as she called the central reservation lines of every hotel chain Richmond Developments had an account with and several it didn't. Thirty minutes later she conceded defeat and passed Logan the second key card to their room.

"I'm tired, and I'm sure you are, too. It's been a busy day. We may as well go and see how bad it is," she said, accepting the inevitable.

The room itself was lovely. Spacious, with a large bathroom and wide windows overlooking a park on the edge of the Willamette River. The bed was exactly as advertised. Queen-size. Honor eyed the carpet and wondered whether she could bear a night sleeping on the floor. Perhaps with a blanket underneath her she could do it.

"Which side do you want?" Logan asked, setting his small suitcase on the floor.

"Side?"

"Of the bed."

"Um…" She stared at the bed and then at him. He wasn't small. Over six feet tall and with shoulders like an Olympic swimmer, he'd take up a fair bit of room. "Look, I can sleep on the floor. If I fold up the bed-cover and make it into a mattress, I'm sure I'll be fine."

"Fine?" He cocked his eyebrow in that ridiculously sexy way of his again. "Don't be silly. We have another busy day tomorrow. If you don't get a good night's sleep, you won't be able to jump high enough when Douglas issues his next imperative."

She detected a note of distaste in his voice. "Not a fan of your newfound father?"

"Not all his business methods, no. My own manage-ment style is less confrontational. But I can live with having opinions that differ from his on a few things. And I can stick to my side of the bed, too. Since you don't seem to want to make a decision, I'll sleep on the window side, okay? You can take the side closest to the bathroom."

He made it sound so simple, Honor almost thought she could do this. In fact, she darn well could do this. Sleeping on the floor was for kids at a sleepover. She was an adult in command of herself in all things. And if she said it long enough and firmly enough, she might even begin to believe it.

"Maybe we can roll up the bedspread and put it down the middle between us," she suggested hopefully.

"Sure, whatever rocks your boat."

He rocked her boat. And that was the problem. No, *she* was the problem.

Keaton. She had to think of him. She had to keep the glimmer of hope that they might work things out in the forefront of her mind at all times. It wasn't such an impossible ask. Despite what he'd said last night about taking a break, she knew he'd be justifiably upset if he found out she and Logan were sharing a room, no matter how innocently it had come about. Would he understand it was a circumstance out of their control? Did he even need to know?

She hated that she was in turmoil like this, second-guessing every thought and feeling. Logan Parker unsettled her on every score.

"Did you want to head out somewhere for dinner to discuss what we looked at today and where we want to focus tomorrow?" Logan suggested, oblivious to the thoughts racing around in her crazy head.

"Sure," she quickly agreed.

It would certainly be better than having room service. The less time they spent together in the confines of this room, the better, no matter how perfectly it was appointed.

"You want to grab a shower first?" Logan asked.

"Thanks, I'll only be a minute."

"Take your time," he said, kicking off his shoes and stretching out on his side of the bed.

For some stupid reason she couldn't help the blush that rose to her cheeks as she watched him. Seeing him like that felt unbearably intimate, but then her stomach rumbled, reminding her that they'd skipped lunch today while touring the property and that it had been a very long time since breakfast. She riffled through her case and grabbed the long-sleeved designer T-shirt and jeans she always kept ready to go for situations like this. Casual enough for downtime on her own, yet smart enough—teamed with a pair of heels, some chunky jewelry and her warm coat—to wear to dinner at a restaurant.

When she emerged from the bathroom, fully dressed, with her face scrubbed free of makeup and her hair freshly washed and blow-dried, Logan appeared to be asleep on the bed. His breathing was slow and even and his features had relaxed from the slightly stern look he sometimes wore. While he was definitely more laid-back than Keaton, she had seen glimpses of the hard strength he would have needed to get where he was today. And, while it was easy to think of him as the underdog given the situation with his family, she'd learned he was a powerful player in New Zealand's business world.

"You all done?" he murmured.

She realized he'd been watching her stare at him.

"Yes, bathroom's all yours."

He moved off the bed and grabbed a couple of items from his case before shutting himself in the steamy confines of the bathroom she'd just vacated. Try as she might, she couldn't suppress the visions that plagued her as she imagined him under the hot spray of the shower. She didn't have to struggle with herself for too long, though, because within four minutes he was back out, dressed and smelling all too enticingly fresh.

"That was quick," she commented as she picked up her bag and headed toward the door.

"Yeah, well, y'know. Guys."

There was absolutely no answer to that, she thought, as they headed out for their meal. The pizza joint they settled on was noisy and busy and just the kind of thing she needed to avoid having to make too much conversation with Logan—even work conversation was difficult. Since they were hungry, they made short work of their dinner. Which meant they were left with time on their hands when they were done.

"Shall we have a drink back at the hotel?" Honor suggested as Logan picked up the tab. "Finish our discussion?"

"Sure, I could kill a beer," Logan said.

It was cold out, and the air around them misted on their breath. They walked side by side back to the hotel, their arms occasionally brushing as they continued along the sidewalk. Honor tried to ignore the sensations aroused in her and kept increasing the distance between them, but the world was full of lampposts, hydrants and other pedestrians that, to her eternal irritation, kept pushing them back together. Even the brightly lit holiday displays all around them couldn't soften her mood.

Man, if she couldn't even walk alongside him without touch being an issue, how on earth was she going to sleep tonight? It was a relief to enter the lobby of the hotel and to be able to put that necessary space between them again. In the bar, Logan ordered a pale ale and she ordered a glass of champagne. The waitress brought their drinks over to where they sat in a secluded corner.

Honor worked hard to keep their conversation focused on work and what they had to do tomorrow. They were both on the same page with their vision for the property, which made things a lot easier. She couldn't help wondering if Keaton would have been so easy to work with. He had a habit of wanting to take the opposing side of any argument, whether he personally supported it or not. She'd always put that down to his stint on the college debate team and had frequently teased him about it, but in this situation it was definitely a whole lot less stressful to easily reach agreement on their objectives.

"We're going to recommend Douglas make that offer, aren't we?" Logan said after finishing the last of his beer.

"It would be foolish not to. Especially if he's serious about expanding into repurposing versus demolition. To be honest, I'm surprised he was so open to the suggestion."

"He's a businessman. He can see that we can charge premium prices for both the commercial and the residential sides if we refurbish what's already there."

"That's what you do in New Zealand, is it? Aim for the premium market?"

"Absolutely. There's a huge demand for repurposing worldwide. Bigger and newer isn't always better, and if we can reconstruct in an ecologically sustainable way, then all the better. Obviously I'd like to see more affordable housing for lower-income families, too, and we're working on that back home."

Their conversation expanded to the potential of green building practices, and Honor felt excited to be able to share her ideas with someone of a like mind. But all of a sudden, she caught herself yawning widely.

"Oh, heavens. I'm sorry, that was rude of me."

"Not at all. You look tired, and I don't mean that in an unkind way. We've had a full day and have another ahead of us tomorrow. Why don't you go to the room? I'm going to sit back, have another beer and come up a bit later. Okay?"

She nodded and all but scurried from the bar. She'd wondered how they were going to manage the whole bedtime routine together, so his suggestion made everything much simpler. And, with any luck, she could even be fast asleep before he came back to the room.

Ten beers wouldn't have been enough to dull his hunger for the woman he was about to sleep with—in the literal sense only, he reminded himself. She'd been so skittish today it had been all he could do not to grab her by the shoulders and kiss her soundly, just to get this crackling tension that bristled between them out of the air. But he'd promised her and, even more importantly, he'd promised his brother that there was nothing to worry about between them. And nothing meant exactly that.

No sweet taste of her lips. No swallowing the sighs and moans she made as he touched her delectable body.

And certainly no losing himself in the slick heat of her as he had when they'd made love.

Damn. And now he had a hard-on.

At least she'd be asleep when he got to the room. He'd waited in the bar long enough. Weariness pulled at every muscle in his body. He'd never understood how much strain it could put a person under to be with someone and yet try not to be with them at the same time. It was the kind of game he'd never wanted to play—never had to, to be honest. But he was a man of his word. He was not going to touch her, no matter how much he craved her.

It was dark in the room when he let himself in. Honor had left the bathroom light on and the door slightly ajar, though, so he wasn't entirely blind when he entered. He went to the bathroom and got ready for bed, realizing too late that he'd brought no pajamas. He'd have to sleep in his boxer briefs—and hopefully keep some measure of circumspection between him and Honor.

She moaned slightly as he slipped beneath the sheets. He stretched out one foot, tentatively seeking to discover if she'd put some kind of barrier between them and smiled as his foot touched what was very obviously a rolled-up towel down the middle of the bed. He pulled back, closed his eyes and lay on his back, willing himself to sleep.

Of course, it was impossible. Instead he lay there, listening to Honor's breathing, feeling the warmth that poured off her body as she slept. Slept, yes, but not peacefully. Every now and then she made a sound of distress, as if she was caught in a bad dream and couldn't verbalize what it was that she needed to say. The noises that came from her were indistinct but clearly unhappy. And then she twitched. An almighty jerk that yanked the covers from him as she burrowed deeper into her side of the bed, still making those noises.

"Honor?" he said gently.

He couldn't just lie here and do nothing. She was obviously upset. Maybe because he was here, but maybe because of something else. Whatever it was, he had the power to wake her and release her from the grip of whatever it was that distressed her. He reached a hand over to touch her lightly on the shoulder and called her name again.

"Honor!" he said more loudly. "Everything's okay. It's just a dream."

She mumbled something that sounded like "no." He could feel her thrashing her head from side to side. This obviously called for more direct contact. He reached out again, this time taking a firm hold on her shoulder, giving her a slight shake and repeating what he'd just said.

He knew the exact moment she was awake from the way her breathing went from rapid and shallow to a sharp gasp followed immediately by a deep sigh. She reached for him, burrowed in tight to his chest as if seeking comfort. Without thinking, Logan wrapped her in his arms and held her tight. Her shoulders shook and he could feel moisture on his bare chest. She was crying? Hell. What kind of dream had it been?

He stroked her hair, her shoulders, her back. Anything to try and soothe away whatever had driven her to this point. And she held on to him tighter than before. Even with that damned rolled-up towel there, he couldn't help his physical reaction. No matter which way he turned, he wanted her, but he knew that it was inappropriate now. Hell, it was inappropriate, period. She was engaged to his brother. He didn't care about the fact that she and Keaton hadn't been intimate in months. It was none of his business. *She* was none of his business. And yet, here she was, in his arms.

And then she kissed him.

Nine

Honor breathed in the scent of Logan's skin, telling herself it was purely to soothe her fractured senses, but somehow even her brain wouldn't accept that truth. Not when her blood pounded through her veins at the nearness of him. Not when his every breath made her breasts press against his chest with enough delicious pressure to make her nipples harden into tight points.

The dream had been a repeat of so many she'd had. Its roots were burrowed deep in her childhood memories and the sense of abandonment she'd always felt even though her mom had never physically left her. Well, not for more than three days at a time, anyway. But she wasn't going to go there again. It was beyond time to put the past to rest, but whenever she was stressed, the old loneliness and fear came surging back, forcing her to seek distraction.

She poured everything she had into that kiss. Everything she'd ever wanted to be. Everything she'd lost. And she had lost. She knew now there was no going back. Doing this, with Logan, meant she was closing a door forever on a future with Keaton.

It was a conscious choice and one she should have made after she'd discovered who Logan Parker was. Whether they went anywhere from here was something she wouldn't think about tonight.

Honor yanked the towel out from between them and slipped one hand over his hip, her palm skimming against the waistband of his briefs and lower to his thigh. No matter what she told herself, it all kept coming back to the same thing. She wanted him. Right here, right now. And more than that she wanted the escape that losing herself in him and the pleasure that she knew they'd find together would bring.

She let her hand slide upward to his chest, feeling his nipples tighten into hard discs before she skimmed her hand down over the taut muscles of his belly and back down to the waistband of his boxers. His hand caught hers, holding her firmly by the wrist and preventing her from reaching her goal as he pulled away from her kiss.

"Are you sure about this?" he asked, his voice thick with desire.

She answered without allowing herself to think. "Yes."

She kissed him again and felt his grip on her hand

loosen, allowing her to continue to touch, to explore. He was hard and hot and so ready she couldn't help the groan of need that came from deep inside her as her fingers closed around him. They'd gone past the point of no return. She needed to be with him just as she needed to breathe. It was instinctual. It was necessary.

His lips and tongue met hers in a fierce duel. The ache at her core became an insistent thrum, demanding she possess him in the most literal sense humanly possible, but now that they'd embarked on this path, she wanted to make it last as long as possible. The first time they'd made love, he'd taken control. Now it was her turn, and she wanted to make the most of it.

Heat poured off his body and she straddled him, lifting off her nightgown and tossing it to the floor beside them. She wanted that heat, craved it, craved him. Inside her, around her, everywhere.

Honor couldn't get enough of the taste of him, let alone the feel of the texture of his skin against her fingertips, her palms. She tugged at his briefs, freed his straining erection and positioned herself to take him into her body. His hands clamped on her hips, holding her in place.

"Protection," he grunted.

"I'm covered," she said.

He groaned as she began to lower onto him, letting her take him inside her at her own pace—slow and steady and with a determination she'd never been so certain of in all her life.

This was what she wanted. No, *needed*. Sensation, pleasure, distraction. No more was she the frightened little girl, or the desperate teen, or the insecure young woman. This—taking power and using it—was what she needed more than anything. And as her body adjusted to his, the ripples of pleasure were already forming. She started to move, at first slowly and then with an increasing frenzy as she reached for completion. Beneath her Logan met her every thrust with one of his own as he reached up to cup her breasts, to tease her rigid nipples and squeeze and mold the soft, full flesh.

"Let go," he urged in a harsh whisper. "Take us both over."

His words were her undoing. She let out a small scream as she relinquished her control over the sensations that had built behind an invisible wall of restraint. There was no more holding back as her climax bloomed from deep inside her. She was vaguely aware of Logan reaching his own, felt his body stiffen and surge and surge again as he came deep inside her. She collapsed onto his chest, both of them slick with perspiration, their breathing heavy, their hearts hammering in their chests.

She lay there hardly believing what she'd just done, exhaustion pulling at every sated muscle. Logan's hand stroked her back, up and down and again, until she felt his body grow slack as he drifted off to sleep. She slid from him and back to her side of the bed, waiting until his breathing was deep and steady before she rose and went to the bathroom, collecting her discarded nightgown on the way.

In the harsh light of the bathroom, she stared at her reflection. Guilt sliced painfully through her. Her gaze dropped to the ring she still wore on her finger, and she tugged it off and slipped it in her toilet bag. She could never wear it again. She would return it to Keaton as soon as she saw him next, along with informing him of her decision that things between them were well and truly over. She'd known it, deep inside, when he'd requested the break, but it hadn't been until she'd woken and reached for Logan that she'd finally accepted it for the truth.

She lifted her eyes to study her face again in the mirror and saw much there to disappoint her. She had the same eyes as her mom, the same shape to her face. The same hair color, even. And the same morals, she thought with a sharp pain in her chest. She really was no different than her mother after all. Ready to throw everything away for a fling with another man and damn the consequences.

Honor quickly washed herself and yanked her nightgown back on before switching off the light and going back to bed. As soon as she was beneath the covers, Logan's arm curled around her waist and pulled her to him. He muttered something in his sleep before settling back into the deep, regular breathing of before. And Honor lay there, taking scant comfort from his presence, unable to sleep as she visualized her entire world disintegrating around her.

As soon as the gray light of dawn began to peep through the windows, Honor bolted from the bed and, grabbing her clothes, went to the bathroom to armor up. She must have had some sleep, she reasoned as she regarded herself in the mirror while brushing her teeth, but not enough to ensure she didn't have deep shadows under her eyes this morning. By the time she'd showered and dressed and returned to the bedroom, Logan was very much awake.

"That your version of the walk of shame?" he challenged, propped up on his pillows with his hands tucked behind his head.

"Bathroom's all yours," she said, ignoring the expanse of bare chest and the question in his eyes, and went to pack her toilet bag and nightgown into her case.

"You're going to ignore what happened between us last night?"

"Why not? Worked last time," she said with fake insouciance.

She saw anger flare in his eyes.

"So that's all I am. A convenient scratching post? We're just going to go back to Seattle today and pretend nothing has happened and you're going to carry on with my brother like last time?"

There was a note of something else in his voice that hadn't been there before. She sighed and turned to face him.

"Keaton and I are on a break, mutually agreed," she said, but before she could continue, he interrupted.

"So what the hell does that mean? You're both free to screw around?"

She flinched at his blunt turn of phrase. He had every right to be angry. She'd messed this up just like she'd messed everything else up along with it.

"No, it doesn't mean that at all. On Sunday night we

agreed to take a break, but when he gets back from his current trip, I'm going to break off our engagement. Obviously, it can't continue. I should have done it immediately after our first night together. What Keaton and I have isn't what he deserves. *I'm* not what he deserves."

"Nor I, apparently. I'm still finding my way with my family. This is going to blow everything apart."

"Why? No one needs to know."

"Seriously? We have sex twice—mind-blowing, soul-searing sex—and you want to pretend it never happened?" He pushed aside the bedcovers and rose from the bed, taking two steps toward her before making a sound of self-disgust and heading for the bathroom.

"Logan, stop."

He stopped but didn't turn around.

Honor took a deep breath. "We can't see one another outside of work. I can't do that to Keaton on top of breaking things off between us."

"But sleeping with me is okay?"

"No, it's not okay." To her horror her eyes filled with tears. "Please, don't say anything about us."

He laughed, and it was a harsh sound. "Oh, don't worry. I got the message. Loud and clear. You're quite safe from me."

The bathroom door closed behind him with a loud snick. Honor took advantage of his absence to finish her packing and, after scrawling a short note to say she'd wait downstairs, she all but ran from the room.

All the way downstairs to the lobby she castigated

herself. Why couldn't she have felt the same way about Keaton as she did for Logan? She'd had her life mapped out. Her future secured. Everything she'd ever wanted had been right there, within her grasp. And she'd messed it up. Two years she'd invested in her relationship with Keaton. Two years of planning together for the life they'd lead. Two years irrevocably down the drain. Her thumb went to the ring finger of her left hand and she felt a jolt of loss when she remembered her engagement ring wasn't there and why.

She was her mother's daughter, no matter which way she looked at it, and the painful truth cut deep.

Honor counted the days until Keaton's return. They'd spoken on the phone a couple of times, but the impending breakup discussion was not the kind of thing you did on the phone. They'd made promises to each other. He deserved her honesty face-to-face. She'd mentioned the trip she and Logan had taken to Portland, mainly because she had a suspicion that Douglas's assistant might let that little gem slip if she was talking to Keaton. The woman was superefficient but garrulous.

Keaton had expressed some shock that she and Logan had been put up in one room after a mix-up, but Honor had impressed on him that it had been a genuine error on Stella's part and that Logan had been a complete gentleman. What she didn't tell him was that she hadn't been a lady. That discussion would have to wait until Keaton's return, and thinking about it had her tied up in knots.

Keaton was due back in the office today, and she'd hoped to see him in private before they came face-to-face in the latest family meeting called by Douglas, but she hadn't been able to catch him. Their talk would clearly have to wait, she thought as she walked to Douglas's office for the urgently called meeting.

While Douglas and Nancy hadn't arrived yet, Logan was already there. Not surprising, she thought, as the man was nothing if not punctual. No, she was being unkind. He was everything *and* punctual with it. She felt the all-too-familiar shock of awareness ripple through her as she saw him standing by one of the large picture windows looking out over the water. And yet again, she wondered why she had never felt this way about Keaton. They were essentially peas in a pod to look at, with the minor exception of Logan having a small chicken pox scar above his right eyebrow. The fact that she'd been close enough to notice and remembered that small detail was another black mark against her.

Honor nodded at Logan, who lifted his chin in acknowledgment of her presence. He'd been scarce in the office these past few days, locked in meetings with Douglas and the architectural team and spending time in the Richmond Developments library studying up on building statutes and related paperwork. He was either being very efficient or he was avoiding her, and she couldn't help but feel it was mostly the latter.

Keaton and Kristin arrived together, their joint laughter a scar on her soul. When was the last time she'd made Keaton laugh? She couldn't even remember. She stepped forward to greet him.

"Welcome home, traveler," she said, giving him a quick hug and a kiss.

Keaton turned his face so her lips landed on his cheek. She knew he wasn't a fan of overt public displays of affection, especially here in the office, but Honor couldn't help but feel perversely slighted by his reaction until she acknowledged the only reason she'd done it was likely to irritate Logan. Which raised the question of why she wanted to irritate him anyway. He'd made it blatantly clear that he wasn't going to pick up his brother's leavings again. When push came to shove, blood was thicker than any attraction they shared and she was good with that, wasn't she?

Douglas and Nancy arrived, and Honor could feel her boss's excitement like a palpable force in the room.

"Good, good. Glad you're all here," Douglas said, rubbing his hands together with obvious glee. "Shame it's too early in the day for champagne, because I have excellent news to share."

"Please, everyone, sit down," Nancy urged them all.

Once they were seated, Douglas turned to Nancy. "You first," he said with a beatific smile on his face.

She gave him a nod then fixed her attention on Logan.

"Logan, we are very pleased and proud to officially welcome you into the family. Your test results are back and you are, without any doubt, our son and Keaton's older twin. I can't begin to tell you how thrilled we are to have you back in the fold." She crossed to Logan, who stood as she enveloped him in her arms. Her voice broke on her next words. "My lost boy, home again. Back where you've always belonged."

Honor watched the tableau before her, her gaze running between mother and son and Keaton and Kristin. Neither of Logan's siblings looked overly thrilled to hear the news. Keaton, in particular, remained stony faced, and when Nancy finally pulled away from Logan, Keaton looked directly at his father.

"So what does that mean going forward, Dad?"

Honor noticed that Keaton's hands had tightened into fists resting on the tops of his thighs. Frustration? Anger? Keaton had a tendency to let irritation and anger take the upper hand from time to time. It was part and parcel of his self-imposed quest to be all and do all to win favor from his father, no doubt. Couldn't he see he was everything Douglas wanted him to be without even trying? He was darn good at his job and would make a great CEO when Douglas stepped down, just as he'd always been groomed to be. But she knew that Keaton had never felt like he was enough.

"I'm glad you asked that, son," Douglas said, rising from his desk. "With Logan coming back to the family and fitting so smoothly into the business dynamic we have running here, I've made some changes in my succession planning."

"What kind of changes?" Kristin demanded.

"Now, now, don't get all worked up. You both know it was always my intention to hand the yoke of control to Keaton. Now, with Logan's return, and given his expertise in the field, it's my wish that he also be considered for contention when I step down."

"What? You have to be kidding!" Keaton shot to his feet and all but shouted at his father. He cast Logan a quick glance. "No disrespect to you, Logan, but you've been here all of five minutes. There's no way you can step in and run the company when Dad steps down. Our corporation is much larger than what you're used to and you haven't spent your entire life being groomed to do this like I have. Dad, this decision is not only grossly unfair to me, it makes very poor business sense. The board of directors are bound to object. Seriously, I beg you to reconsider."

"My mind is made up. You know I plan to retire in two years. That's ample time for Logan to be brought up to speed. Many CEOs have far less when they take on a new role. I know this must be disappointing to you, Keaton, but it is what it is."

"And what about Logan?" Kristin asked, her face now as pale as the white blouse she was wearing under her conservative navy blue suit. "What do you think of all this?"

"I'm shocked, obviously. I hadn't even decided to stay in the States."

"*Hadn't?*" Kristin said, leaping instantly on the most telling word in his statement.

"Yes, hadn't. Until now."

She made a derisive sound. "So, now that you're proven to be one of us, you think you can just romp straight home to the finish line and take over? Just like that?" Kristin turned to her father. Her fury was clearly painted on her face. "How could you? As if it wasn't bad enough that you never even considered me as your replacement, when I have more business acumen in my little finger than Keaton has, period. Now you go and stomp all over him. After all these years of his dogged loyalty to you, this is how you treat him? Frankly, right now, I'm ashamed to be your daughter."

She rose from her seat and stalked out of the room, letting the door bang closed behind her.

Keaton turned his attention back to his father. "I'm going to ask you to reconsider this preposterous idea. Hopefully in a day or two you'll come to your senses. If you don't, I'm going to make a recommendation to the board that you be let go from your position here."

High color flooded Douglas's cheeks. "On what grounds?" he challenged.

"Diminished mental capacity," Keaton said succinctly before following in his sister out of the room.

Ten

Honor was exhausted when she let herself into her apartment that evening. The atmosphere at work had been incredibly strained for the balance of the day after Douglas's announcement. And it hadn't taken long for it to filter out to the rest of the staff, many of whom were shocked that a newcomer could be in line to become their new CEO. To make things worse, she hadn't been able to track Keaton down anywhere. Even his executive assistant had no idea where he'd gone, and he wasn't answering his phone. Honor was beginning to become seriously worried, as she tried for the umpteenth time to reach him, when her doorbell buzzed repeatedly.

She rushed to open the door, knowing it had to be him, and was shocked when he lurched across the threshold, reeking of cigarette smoke and booze. His dark blond hair, normally so tidy, was in complete disarray. His tie was loosened and askew, and there were stains on his suit jacket that hadn't been there this morning.

"You shtill love me, doncha?" he slurred as he slung one arm over Honor's shoulder and hugged her to him.

"Of course I love you," she said.

"At least shomebuddy does," he said, sounding slightly reassured.

But even as the words had fallen from her lips, she knew them to be a lie. Well, not an entire lie. She loved Keaton as she'd love a very good friend. But not the way she ought to have loved him. Not the way he deserved to be loved by someone he'd asked to marry.

She guided him to the couch, where he lay down almost immediately. Honor swiftly removed his shoes and went to the kitchen to grab him a glass of water. She stood at the kitchen counter for a full two minutes, wondering how she was ever going to tell him the truth that he'd been a part of her ticket to a respectable and successful life. That she'd been prepared to accept second best and to force him to do the same. Not for the first time, she wished Logan Parker had never discovered his true identity. Life had been so much simpler before he turned up.

But even so, she couldn't blame him. Her planned future with Keaton had been a hopeless cause, destined to failure, right from the start. Cracks would have formed eventually. At least this way they'd found out before more damage was done. She poured his glass of water and walked back to her sitting room. Keaton was already fast asleep and snoring lightly. Honor looked at him, feeling nothing but compassion fill her heart as she watched him sleep off what she was certain was his very first drunken episode since college.

A man as buttoned up as Keaton never let himself go like this. That his father's announcement today had driven him to this, well, it just made her mad all over again. At Logan Parker for existing. At Douglas Richmond for being such an idiot and so careless with his children's aspirations. And at herself for not loving Keaton better. And somehow she was going to have to find the courage to tell this broken man that she couldn't be engaged to him anymore.

She'd failed in her quest to create the life she'd always wanted, and she knew she certainly could not continue to work at Richmond Developments with Logan Parker eventually at the helm. She'd have to start over again, somewhere else. But as soon as the thought formed in her mind, she felt a corresponding pain in her chest over walking away from the man she now realized she was falling in love with.

Shock drove her to sit down before her legs gave way completely. Love Logan Parker? That was madness. Madness doomed to ultimate failure. So what if she felt an inexorable pull toward him every time she saw him? In fact, right from the very first time she'd laid eyes on him. It was just animal attraction. A primeval itch that needed scratching. And they'd scratched it. Not once, but twice. Each time instigated by her. Each time equally as intense and sexually fulfilling.

That didn't mean she loved him. She couldn't love him. She barely knew him. But the deeper she looked into her heart, the more she knew the truth. It didn't make sense. In fact, it was the most awful realization to reach. But she was in love with Logan. And she could never, ever have him.

Logan was thoroughly pissed off. How could Douglas have made such an announcement without at least running it past him privately first? Sure, he could understand the DNA results being shared with the entire family, but Douglas's harebrained scheme to install him at the head of Richmond Developments?

He paced his hotel room for the hundredth time and threw himself down on the bed when he realized that all this pacing only served to wind him up even more. He needed to run or swim or do something—anything—that would burn up this restless energy and frustration that had clawed at him all day long.

Sex would work, the contrary voice at the back of his mind suggested, but Logan slammed that thought right back where it belonged. There was only one person he wanted sex with, and look how that had turned out so far. No, Honor Gould was so far off-limits she was virtually in another galaxy.

Or just across town, the voice said again.

With a growl of irritation, Logan quickly changed into a pair of shorts, a T-shirt and running shoes and took the elevator to the hotel gym. An hour or ten on the treadmill ought to do it, he thought to himself as he programmed the machine to the highest incline and started to run. But the running didn't help. Even though it wore him out physically, his mind continued to return to Honor. To how she felt, how she tasted, to the little sounds she made when they made love. Made love? No, it was just sex, pure and simple.

Nothing pure about it, came that wretched voice again. Under any other circumstance, he would have enjoyed pursuing the idea of building something with Honor, however, under this circumstance he wasn't going near her again. He'd waited his entire life to be a part of his rightful family. Sleeping with Honor had been a stupid thing to do the first time, but the second confirmed that he was a real fool. He hadn't wanted to do anything that would jeopardize his chances for acceptance within the Richmonds' tight familial group, but his relationship with Honor, along with his father's blasted announcement today, had thrown everything to the wind.

Logan set the treadmill to a cool-down pace, reached for the towel he'd slung over the rail and swiped at the perspiration that beaded his face and throat. His sweaty T-shirt clung to his body. Maybe this was all his fault after all. He had a good life back in New Zealand. He had a family that loved and accepted him there, even if they weren't his blood. He had a thriving company, friends and interests that kept his life full. But for all that he loved those things, none of it filled the hole in his heart where his true family should be.

And now, even though he'd found them and his parents had accepted him wholeheartedly into the family, there was a yawning chasm separating him and his siblings. His twin, whom he should be closest to, now probably wanted nothing to do with him, and his sister, well, the waters ran deep with her. Clearly she'd always felt she was the better candidate to take over their father's role at the company, and equally as clearly, his father had never considered her for the position. Because she was female? Or because he truly had believed Keaton better suited to the role?

When Logan returned to his hotel room, he stripped and stepped into the shower. Keeping the water on a stinging cold temperature, he lathered up, rinsed off and then turned the water up a little. He could turn down Douglas's position, he thought as the water streamed over his body. Or find some way to extend an olive branch to his brother and sister. Maybe find some kind of way to generate a three-way split of the company leadership. Surely they'd be on board with that? He could only try, right?

Wrong.

Logan looked from Kristin to Keaton and back again. His brother looked somewhat the worse for wear; Logan recognized his pallor as that of someone who'd had a few too many drinks and then slept poorly into the bargain. He recognized it because he also had looked like that a time or two. Kristin, well, she was about as buttoned up and tense as a person could be without shattering into tiny splinters all over the meeting room where he'd called them this morning.

"We need to learn to work together," Logan said firmly.

"Or you could just go back to New Zealand and stay there," Kristin said with viperish scorn.

"Oh, he's here to stay, and good luck to him. He'll soon find out that no matter how hard you work, how often you break your back to please, or how many years of your life you give up doing it, Dad will never be satisfied. And, by the way, *bro*, don't think that when he steps down he'll actually be stepping down. He'll be there at your shoulder like the Ghost of Christmas Past. Criticizing, analyzing and interfering, because that's what he does best."

"Rethinking your desire to find your family?" Kristin sneered when Logan didn't immediately respond.

"Look, I can see why my arrival has upset both your lives. It hasn't exactly been a walk in the park for me, either. But I do have just as much right to be here as you do."

"Except you haven't earned your stripes here the way we have," Kristin responded sharply.

"And if I had? What then? Would you hate me any less?" Logan replied with equal sharpness.

Kristin held his gaze for a few seconds then flushed and looked away. "We don't hate you, Logan. How can we? We barely know you."

"And maybe that's the problem here," Logan offered. "We could try harder to get to know one another, don't you think?"

"I guess," Kristin agreed. "What do you think, Keaton? You want to get to know this guy before he becomes our boss?"

Keaton focused his gaze on his brother. "Whatever. I

still don't think he's got what it takes to run this place. It's what I was raised to do. Every choice and every decision I've faced was with that role in mind. I can't believe he chose you."

"I agree," Kristin said, rising from her chair. "And I've always thought I was the better person for the job, because let's face it, I run the money side of things and my grades were always better than yours, plus I'm more of a people person than you are. But better the devil we know, right?"

"I am actually still here in the room," Logan reminded them. "And, to be totally honest with you both, I'm fully capable of running this company as CEO on my own, but—" he raised his hand as they both looked set to argue that point with him "—I would prefer to come to some agreement with you both whereby we work together instead of trying to tear each other down. If you guys can't be on the same page as me with that, then I will work alone. Do you understand me?"

"Do you hear that?" Kristin said, looking at Keaton with a hint of a grin tugging at her lips. "He's got that big brother thing down pat."

"Yeah, I guess we'd better toe the line, huh?" Keaton said with a glimmer of a smile on his face, too.

Logan felt a slight sense of relief until he looked at his brother and felt the dreaded guilt that always filled him whenever he thought about what he'd done with Honor. Sure, the first time had been innocent enough, but the second? No, he couldn't go there. He was surprised, though, that he hadn't heard any news about their engagement being off. He was certain Honor would have followed through on that when they returned from Portland. But then again, he rationalized, would she have had the opportunity with Keaton's travel and then the bombshell yesterday?

He only hoped that when she did finally break that connection with his brother, that she didn't tell Keaton the full reason why. Because if she did, he doubted he'd ever be able to build the kind of relationship with his brother that he wanted. Goodness only knew it was the kind of thing he'd never forgive if the tables were turned. And didn't that just make him feel like he was the lowest of the low.

"So, what do you two say? How about dinner tonight? Just the three of us. Somewhere casual where we can start to really get to know one another."

"Are you paying?" Kristin asked with a raised brow.

"Sure," Logan answered with a smile. "If that's what it takes."

"Then I can make myself available," she answered.

"Me too. But this better not give me indigestion," Keaton said reluctantly.

"A few beers together and you'll be right," Logan said, slapping his brother on the back and earning a sharp glare in return.

"I won't be drinking," Keaton said firmly, before adding under his breath, "ever again."

Logan laughed. "I know what that feels like."

Kristin rolled her eyes as the two of them began to discuss hangover remedies.

"While you two good ol' boys do your reminiscing together, I have work to do. What time tonight, Logan?"

"How about seven?" he suggested. "I saw a place over by Lake Union the other day." He mentioned the name of the restaurant. "I'll make a reservation and see you there."

After they'd gone back to their offices, he felt a glimmer of hope that he might be able to build something of a friendship with his brother and sister after all. Which left one more problem on his horizon. Honor. Sharing an office with her was no longer an option. Yes, they may have to liaise with one another on a regular basis, but there was no real need for them to be within the same workspace, day in and day out, was there? He'd check if that office refit on the architectural design team's floor was complete.

But a week later, he discovered it wasn't as easy to relocate as he'd hoped. Plus, he began to see a different side to Honor here in the office. She was intensely focused and had some very strong and worthwhile opinions on his vision for the Portland contract.

"Look, I see where you're going with this," she said to him on the Friday morning the week before Christmas. "And while I applaud what you're trying to do here, I think we'd be better if we went for a more industrial look for the interiors of the stores and restaurants. Not only would it shave costs, but it would add to the overall aesthetic of the entire courtyard precinct we'll be developing."

He nodded and leaned in a little closer to the concept drawings she had spread out on the table in front of them. It was dangerous ground. The nearer he got to Honor, the more tantalizing was her scent. He had to school himself not to want to nuzzle against the side of her neck and breathe in deep. Easier said than done, he acknowledged as she shifted slightly, giving him an all-too-enticing view of the lace of her bra peeking out from just inside the neckline of her top. Red. The color of passion.

Logan forced himself to train his eyes on the sketches and studied them as though his life depended on it. But it was no use. Her nearness, the warmth of her body as she leaned over the table and scribbled something on the drawing in front of them—all of it conspired to fry his brain and heat up other parts of his body that had no business getting heated in the workplace.

"Logan?"

He started a little and realized she'd been talking to him.

"Sorry, could you repeat that?"

She sighed a little, the action making the fabric of her top shift a little, and darn it if he didn't catch another little peek of ruby-red lace.

"Look, maybe it'd be easier if I just took you out to a place about half an hour away that illustrates what I'm talking about."

He stifled a groan. A half hour in a car with her there and then another back? It would be sheer torture.

"Sounds good to me," he heard himself saying.

"Are you free to go now?"

"Sure."

"You know, when you first came here and started espousing your ideas about preserving the history of a lot of these old buildings, I thought you were mad. I'd always adhered to Douglas's policy of making a fresh start, especially when it came to housing. But I really love your ideas of creating homes for families and space for small businesses out of these old industrial buildings. You're creating new community hubs and giving people an opportunity to connect on a personal level with family and friends that we don't tend to see very often these days."

She actually sounded really excited about what they were doing, and Logan felt a burst of pride that she'd come around to his way of thinking and without too much effort on his part. But underneath the excitement he heard a wistful note in her voice that made him curious. As if she had some hidden pain stuffed down deep inside. It was unusual for her to show a chink in her armor, and it made him all the more curious to know exactly what made her tick.

"Are you close to yours?" he asked.

"My what?"

"Your family."

She stiffened and pulled a slight face. "Not at all. My father left us when I was about six or seven. And my mom is in a care facility now. Alcohol-related dementia."

She said the words as if she was reciting a shopping list but Logan could hear the wealth of hurt behind them.

"I'm sorry."

She shrugged as if it didn't matter. "It is what it is. Shall we go?"

Subject firmly closed, he acknowledged silently as he followed her. With all she'd left unsaid, he knew her childhood couldn't have been easy. But maybe it explained why he'd heard nothing yet about her breaking off her engagement. Had she changed her mind about that? Was her own past the reason why she was clinging to the security a future with Keaton would offer? After all, it wasn't as if he could offer her the same. Or could he?

Eleven

Honor drooped with weariness when she let herself into her apartment that evening. She usually felt drained by Friday evening because she put so much into her work week. But this week had been especially taxing. Spending time with Logan challenged her on every level and left her feeling like a wound-up spring of tension by the end of each day. He was so…everything. It irritated her that he was really good at his job, even though Douglas hadn't bestowed an official title on him yet. And he was always open to ideas, as today's trip had proven. He'd been really impressed with the site she'd taken him to, and when they got back to the office he'd been excited about working her suggestions into the concepts for the Portland project. His enthusiasm had been infectious, and she'd even found herself enjoying his company in a way she'd never believed she'd be capable of with all that lay between them.

And what lay between them was just as strong as it had ever been. He was like a magnet for her, and she was little more than a metal filing inexorably drawn to him at every turn. She could only hope that in time she'd inure herself to the crazy way her body reacted to him. Surely frequent contact would eventually de-sensitize her, right?

She'd struggled to find the right time to have that talk with Keaton. And it wasn't just because she was reluctant to have it. Pinning him down for the discussion had proven more difficult than she'd anticipated. He'd been away at a golfing tournament the previous weekend and then involved in negotiations with overseas suppliers all this week, which had, in turn, required him to wine and dine the suppliers' representatives every night.

Honor kicked off her shoes and sank down onto her couch. She remembered just how vulnerable Keaton had appeared last week after Douglas's announcement appointing Logan as his successor. It had been as though Keaton's entire reason for being had been stripped from him. It would have been cruel of her to end their engagement on top of all of that. But now that he seemed to be coming to terms with Logan's permanent place in the family, the time to discuss this with him had to be now and tonight he'd agreed to call in.

She had to release him from their engagement. She got up from the couch, went to her kitchen and poured herself a glass of wine.

She was just about to take a sip when her apartment door buzzed. Keaton. She felt a sudden sense of trepidation. Honor put down her glass and after pasting a smile on her face, swung open the door.

"Keaton, I was literally just thinking about you."

"Thinking about me? Are you sure you didn't confuse me with my brother? You two can't seem to stop looking at one another. I thought it was just him, but you're just as bad."

She felt as shocked as if he'd slapped her. His voice was sharp with an edge of something cruel lingering under the surface that she'd never heard from him before.

"You'd better come in," she said, stepping aside for him to enter.

"You don't deny it, I see."

"Please, sit down."

She sat opposite him. Despite the fact his features were so very familiar to her, he had the air of a complete and utter stranger. His mouth was set in an implacable line, and his eyes were icy and unforgiving.

"Am I right?" he asked coldly. "Is there something between you and my brother?"

Her mouth went dry, and she felt nauseous that Keaton had guessed the truth. She'd wanted to spare him that. She'd wanted to end their engagement in as civilized a fashion as possible, without imparting just how foolish she'd been.

"I'm sorry, Keaton, I—"

"I'll take that as a yes," he ground out through clenched teeth.

Keaton closed his eyes briefly, and she saw his chest rise and fall as he drew in a deep breath, as if he was trying to steady himself. Twin spots of color stained his cheeks red, a sure sign it was one of those rare moments when his temper truly got away with him.

"I can explain," she started, but Keaton put up one hand.

"Don't insult me with your explanations. They're too little, too late as far as I'm concerned. I can't believe it took me this long to see you for what you really are."

"What am I?"

Honor's voice sounded thick and strained, even to her ears.

"I knew you were ambitious. I liked that about you, more fool me. But I never realized that you'd be prepared to play my brother and me. I imagine now that Logan's set to take over from our father, you'll shift your allegiance to him as he has by far the most to gain."

"That's not true. Not at all!" she protested. "Keaton, honestly, the first time—"

"There's been more than one?" he asked, sounding shocked.

Honor swallowed the bitter taste in her mouth. He deserved the whole truth.

"Please, Keaton, hear me out. You need to know everything."

"I'm not sure I do."

"Look, the night of the awards dinner I was in the hotel bar and I was just about to go up to my room when I saw a man I believed was you come into the bar and take a seat."

"But I told you I couldn't make it to your award presentation. Why would you have thought he was me?"

"You're identical twins. Honestly, I really thought that maybe you'd come into town to surprise me with some role play."

"Role play," he repeated, his voice now devoid of any emotion.

"You know we'd had a discussion about spicing things up. I thought maybe you'd taken that on board. Anyway—" she waved a hand in the air in front of her "—I thought he was you. I went over to him. Kissed him. Gave him my room number and key card and asked him to join me."

"And he did." Keaton's face was stony.

Retelling the story just made it sound all the more sordid.

"So you slept with him that night, too? And Portland? The shared room? Was that something the two of you engineered?"

"No!" she cried. "Stella made the reservation thinking I was traveling with you, and when the hotel only had the one room left, we had no choice but to share it."

"Even so, you didn't have to have sex with him."

She hung her head in shame. "I know. I couldn't help it."

Keaton made a sound halfway between grief and disgust and then rose abruptly.

"Well, I wish you luck. Obviously, I have no further interest in continuing our engagement."

"I'll get your ring."

"You haven't been wearing it?"

"I couldn't. Not after Portland. It…it wasn't right."

"No, it wasn't. None of this was."

"Are you going to tell your parents and Kristin?"

"About you screwing my brother? I don't think so. Life's bad enough without them knowing that, too."

Her chest felt as if it was being compressed in a vise. "Thank you," she whispered.

Honor left him waiting in the sitting room while she went to retrieve the diamond solitaire she'd been so proud to accept. When she came back and handed it to him, she felt as if she was returning everything she'd ever strived for. Stability. Security. Structure. Acceptance. And with her own ridiculous carelessness, she'd thrown it all away.

Keaton took the ring, pocketed it and turned and left without saying another word. The moment the door closed behind him, Honor crumpled to the floor and began to cry. Great wrenching sobs shook her entire body and, when they eventually subsided, left her feeling broken and empty in a way she'd never felt before. She staggered to her feet and grabbed the glass of wine from her coffee table. She lifted it to her mouth with a shaking hand but then stopped herself.

How many times had she seen her mother turn to alcohol for comfort when life went wrong? She would not be like that. Honor walked to the kitchen and tipped the wine out in the sink before heading to her bedroom and lying down on her bed, in the dark and fully clothed.

She waited for sleep to come, but it was impossible.

Her mind was full of all the things she and Keaton had done and planned together. All the times his family had included her as though she was one of them and had value and importance. She couldn't expect to experience that again. She was a cheater. The worst kind. Just like her father and just like her mom.

Honor curled up on her side and let the tears fall again. This time she wept silently, feeling her heart break into a million pieces as she cried for all she'd destroyed. She cried for the little girl who'd had hopes and dreams of a better life and who'd wanted to be loved and accepted for herself. Who'd wanted to make a difference for others. Who'd wanted to be a part of something greater than who she was and where she'd been and what she'd done.

The girl who'd ruined everything.

By Monday morning, Honor still wasn't certain she could face the others. She'd be a pariah once the news came out. There'd be no one in her corner, especially not Logan. He'd already made it clear that he wanted nothing to do with her on a personal level. And that was as it should be, too. His family situation was too fragile and new and precious. If she'd been in the same situation, she'd do the same.

Family was everything. If you had it.

She felt another wave of pain, and she gripped the edges of her vanity table so tightly her fingers began to hurt. She couldn't face going in to work today. She'd just call in sick. And how long could she continue to do that, she silently asked her reflection. No, she had to go in and face the music.

How long would it be, she wondered, until she was asked to leave Richmond Developments? It was bound to happen eventually. The family was tight, even with their infighting, and eventually they'd discover that she'd overstepped the invisible boundaries that held a family together. She'd do the right thing and resign. Maybe then she might still be able to expect a reference. She'd been good at her job, had helped lift the company profile. Surely she'd have no difficulty finding work elsewhere. Her portfolio was impressive.

But her financial commitments were extensive, and she couldn't take a hit right now. Not only was she still paying down her student loans, but the care facility where her mother now lived consumed most of her financial resources. Job security was vital for her to be able to make those payments for her mom. Sure, Honor could maybe move to a cheaper apartment, sell her car and take public transit. But that wouldn't make much difference for long.

She was going to have to take stock of her life, her new life, and make contingency plans like tightening her budget, creating a new résumé and registering with some employment agencies. Then she would have to wait and see what happened next.

Over the next two days at work, Honor felt as though she was perpetually walking on eggshells. It was the Tuesday before Christmas, and the atmosphere in the office should have been festive and joyful. Maybe for the rest of the staff it was, but between the Richmond siblings, and between herself and Logan, you could cut the tension with a knife.

Keaton barely spoke to anyone, and Kristin was so tightly wound she was like a bomb waiting to go off. And Logan? Well, he was very creative at finding ways not to be anywhere near her, until now as they exited the conference room after attending a department heads meeting. When he went to speak with Keaton, she was horrified to see his brother cut him dead in the hallway and turn and walk away without acknowledging him.

"What was that about?" Logan asked as he and Honor walked along the corridor.

"He hasn't spoken to you?"

Logan made a helpless gesture with his hands. "As you can see, he isn't talking to me. Not even to say good morning. Not sure what bug has crawled up his ass, but I thought we were making inroads into getting to know one another. Now this. Has he always been so moody?"

Honor shook her head. "It's my fault. Well, *our* fault."

"Ours?"

She watched as understanding dawned on his face.

"You told him?"

"I did." Even as she said the words, she felt the now-familiar nausea from knowing she'd inflicted such humiliating pain on Keaton.

"He didn't take it well, did he?" Logan cursed under his breath. "I'm so sorry you bore that alone. We should have told him together."

She looked at him in surprise. "No, it was my responsibility."

"Honor, we were both involved. I should have been there for you. I'm sorry."

The reality that she'd been the instrument of her own demise hit home all over again, crushing the air from her lungs and making her stumble a little as she walked. Logan instantly put out a hand to steady her, and the warmth of his touch filtered through her blouse to her arm. She pulled away, when all she wanted to do was revel in his touch. To take the comfort he offered and let it heal the darkness inside her.

"Still can't keep your hands off each other I see," Kristin sniped as she passed them in the hallway.

Kristin flung Logan a look laced with disgust and continued on her way. Honor closed her eyes briefly and groaned. This was impossible. Obviously Keaton had talked to Kristin. And if he'd told her, who else knew? This was turning into a disaster. The strife she'd caused with her careless and reckless behavior, and her inability to keep a sensible distance between herself and the temptation that was Logan Parker, was causing a rift between the reunited siblings that was wider and deeper than anything she could ever have imagined.

Simply by remaining here at Richmond Developments, she was making everything so much worse than it needed to be. She had no doubt they'd forgive Logan in time, but no one would ever forgive her. And, as much as that hurt, she had to admit that if the situation was reversed and this was her family that was being ripped apart, she'd be reacting exactly the same way.

But there was something she could do to make it right. She could step away. By doing so it would clear the path to allow the siblings to find their way back to each other without her presence being a constant reminder of the wedge she'd driven between Logan and Keaton. She had to at least try to make something right here.

Honor stopped in her tracks.

"What's wrong?" Logan asked.

"There's something I need to do. You go on. I'll be in touch later about the cost analysis for the local waterfront restaurant and boutique complex."

Before he could say anything else, she turned around and went back the way she'd come, heading directly for Douglas's office. She nodded to Stella as she entered the inner sanctum.

"The boss man free?" she asked.

"He doesn't have anyone with him right now, but—"

"Good," Honor said firmly and continued to his office door.

She rapped her knuckles on the wood, and without waiting for him to answer, she let herself in. Douglas was sitting at his desk. He didn't look too good as he lifted his head and acknowledged her.

"Honor, to what do I owe the pleasure? I hope everything is okay?"

"I've come to give you my resignation," she said without preamble.

Douglas rose from his chair and walked around his desk. He took her hands in his.

"Now, which one of my boys has upset you? I'll deal

with it. There's no need for you to resign over some petty argument."

"The thing is, Douglas, this isn't a petty argument. I've done something really stupid, and I'm the only person who can do anything to fix it."

Then, to her absolute horror, she burst into tears. Douglas led her over to the sofas that faced one another on one side of his office.

"There, there," he said, looking more uncomfortable by the minute. "I'm sure it can't be that bad."

"It's worse. I slept with Logan. I thought he was Keaton but he wasn't and now Keaton knows and our engagement is off and they're not talking and Kristin thinks I'm evil and I just can't stay here anymore."

Douglas listened to her crazy run of words and reached into his pocket. He withdrew a clean white handkerchief, shook it open and passed it to her. She blindly took the square of cotton, wiped her eyes and unceremoniously blew her nose.

"I'm sorry," she said through tears. "I didn't mean to dump all that on you that way, but it's the truth. I did a stupid thing, and the only way I can make it right is by leaving."

Douglas looked at her, his expression serious. "We can work this out. People make mistakes. Some of us more than others," he said with a somewhat wistful look in his eyes.

"I can't stay here and be a constant reminder to them both. I need to move on. I'm sorry I was unfaithful to Keaton. You know how much I was looking forward to marrying him and being a true part of your family, but I had to admit that I didn't love him enough to do that. I didn't love him enough to recognize that it wasn't him that I slept with three weeks ago."

And she hadn't loved him enough not to repeat the experience in Portland less than a week later.

"Let me talk to him," Douglas offered.

"No, it won't make any difference, and nor should it. I betrayed him, Douglas. I betrayed his trust with the brother he has spent his whole life trying to make up for."

"Make up for? Why? Keaton has always been a source of great pride to Nancy and me."

Douglas looked affronted. No, not affronted exactly, but not right, either. Something was bothering him deeply, and Honor felt even guiltier that she was the one heaping additional stress on him.

"I know he has, but he's always felt he had to be more because of the one you lost. He never felt like he was enough."

Douglas got up and began to pace the room. "That's ridiculous. He never said anything to—" He put his hand to his head and grimaced. "This damn headache just won't go away."

"I'll get you something. Look, I'm sorry to have offloaded on you like that, but I mean it about resigning. I'll give you my written letter this afternoon, and I'd like to finish up as quickly as possible."

He looked at her, and to her horror, his gaze went completely blank before his eyes closed and he dropped to the carpet in a crumpled heap. Honor rocketed to her feet and ran to him, kneeling at his side. He wasn't breathing. She put her fingers to his neck, desperate to feel his pulse, but there wasn't even so much as a flutter.

"Stella, help!" Honor yelled. "I need help. Call for a paramedic!"

When Stella opened the office door, Honor was already doing chest compressions, but somehow she knew, in her heart, that it was a waste of time. She'd watched the man die right in front of her. She'd seen the life dull then disappear from his eyes. Worse, she'd been the one to ensure his last moments were filled with worry and regret.

Twelve

Logan stood in the outer office together with his brother, sister and Nancy, as Douglas's covered body was wheeled away. Kristin began to sob quietly, and Logan put an arm around her, offering her solace. Stella was quietly crying at her desk. Honor stood, leaning against the wall, her face pale and drawn, and her arms wrapped around her middle as if she'd fall apart if she let go.

He ached to comfort Honor but his sister needed him too, which left him feeling utterly torn. Honor looked shattered and so desperately alone in this moment and he knew she had to be grieving too. That, combined with the shock of being with Douglas when he died so suddenly must have been really tough to deal with. He'd heard she'd worked tirelessly, performing CPR until the paramedics had arrived.

He felt cold and numb inside. And cheated. He was only just beginning to know his father, and now the man had been taken from him. Keaton was holding their mother in a tight hug, and Logan could see how she shook as grief racked her body.

The paramedics who'd attended Douglas came through from the office—all their equipment packed up, somber expressions on their faces. One of the men stopped by Nancy and Keaton.

"We're sorry for your loss, ma'am."

"Thank you. I know you all did everything you could," she said on a choked sob that cut right through Logan's heart.

The silence in the room was near deafening once the medical professionals had departed. One of the police officers who'd attended the 9-1-1 call talked briefly to Keaton and Nancy, explaining the procedure with the coroner's office.

"Since we've spoken with Mr. Richmond's doctor and his vascular neurologist and they've confirmed his medical situation, it should be a fairly straightforward procedure with the autopsy. They'll be in touch with you regarding the release of his body."

"Thank you, Officer. So, we are free to leave now?" Keaton asked.

"Of course, and my condolences on your loss."

"Thank you. C'mon, Mom, I'll see you home. There's nothing we can do here."

"We'll have to start making arrangements, letting people know," Nancy said, a note of hysteria coloring her voice.

"Not yet, Mom," Kristin said, pulling free of Logan's embrace and crossing to her mother. "Soon, but not yet. I'll come with you two."

"And Honor?" Nancy asked, reaching out a hand in Honor's direction.

"No, Mom, not Honor," Keaton said firmly.

Keaton's dismissal of Honor's right to be a part of the family at this time cut Logan like a jagged knife. Honor deserved compassion, too. Logan wanted nothing more than to say he'd join them as well, but something in the set of Keaton's shoulders and the expression on his face made it abundantly clear he was not welcome, either.

Kristin met Logan's gaze. "Are you coming with us?" she asked, ignoring how Keaton stiffened beside her in silent protest.

"I'll see that Stella and Honor are taken care of and try to join you later, okay?"

Kristin nodded, and Logan watched as his brother and sister shepherded Nancy from the office toward the elevators, and his heart ached for the man they had all lost so abruptly. He'd spent his whole life feeling as though he didn't quite belong and he'd thought it would be different with his own blood relatives. How wrong could he have been? He'd never felt more of an outsider in his own family than he did right now. The others had drawn together in a way that had excluded him. They shared memories with the man who'd been such a powerful force in their lives—the person who had knitted them all together. Logan was no more than the new guy on the block, no matter what the DNA results had said.

He looked at Honor. "You okay?" he asked.

"I…he…he just dropped right in front of me. There was nothing I could do."

Silent tears began to streak down her face, and her entire body shook. He couldn't help but draw her against him in an all-encompassing hug of compassion. When she began to calm again, he reluctantly let her go.

"Let me see that Stella has a support person and then I'll take you home. You can't drive yourself in this state."

He called HR and asked for someone to come and stay with Stella until a family member could be reached to collect her, and he asked that Honor's coat and bag be collected from her office so she wouldn't have to face anyone else just yet. She wasn't in any state to field questions.

As soon as the HR staffer arrived with Honor's things and to attend to Stella, he tucked Honor's arm in his and began to lead her away. She immediately tugged clear of him.

"I'll be fine," she said.

But there was a tone in her voice that said she was anything but. The need to care for her overtook everything else and Logan quickly fell into step beside her. She was so brittle right now he was concerned she'd fracture into a tiny million pieces. Several other staff members looked up as they passed, a mix of shock and sympathy on their faces. It hadn't taken long for the news of Douglas's death to spread through the office.

"Give me your keys," he commanded as they headed for the elevators.

She did so without another murmur of objection, and that worried him more than anything. As they waited for the car to get to their floor, he looked around. The decorations festooning the office had never looked more garish and overdone than they did at this moment. Christmas. A time for joy and sharing, but for the Richmond family, it would forever be a time marked by loss as well.

When they reached the parking garage, they walked to Honor's car. He hit the unlock on the remote and opened her door for her. She settled into the seat with a softly murmured thank-you.

Once he was behind the wheel, with the seat and mirror adjusted for his far greater height, he turned to her. "I'll need you to give me directions."

In answer, she tapped on the navigation app on the dashboard screen and hit a location. Taking that as a very strong hint that she wasn't up to talking, Logan put the car in gear and followed the directions issued by the disembodied voice through the speakers.

Traffic was heavy as he negotiated through the streets. People everywhere scurried around wrapped in hats, scarves and coats, obviously eager to get out of the elements. The sky, as usual, was thick with heavy, gray, low clouds, and drifts of rain kept the roads slick with moisture. At four o'clock in the afternoon, it was getting dark already.

He'd never felt so far from home as at this moment. Back in New Zealand it was sunny, warm and humid and people were in shorts, T-shirts and flip-flops already. This flip side of his reality felt more foreign than he'd ever realized. Did he even really belong here?

He'd thought he did, but the way things were turning out, maybe he ought to just cut his losses and head home to New Zealand. To the heat of summer, to the family where he'd never quite fit in, to his business and new opportunities there. But even as he considered all those things as he drove through the busy streets, he knew he wouldn't—no, *couldn't*—quit on his family here or on Honor. His feelings for her were complicated but he thrived on that. He'd find a way to make it work—to make *them* work. Somehow.

After parking Honor's car in her underground parking garage and escorting her to her door, he was feeling about as wrecked as she looked. He'd get a cab back to his hotel, lock himself in his room and take a long, hot shower to try to chase away the chill that had invaded his body right to the marrow.

"Will you be okay?" he asked as Honor opened her apartment door.

"I guess," she answered in a voice that was little more than a whisper. "How about you?"

He shrugged. Words defeated him right now, and a solid lump of emotion had taken up residence in his throat.

"Logan? Do you want to come in for a while? I can make some coffee, or something stronger, if you'd like?"

She sounded lost, alone and desperate for the company. Much how he felt, too. And despite thinking he was ready to leave her and dwell alone on his loss,

he found that he wasn't quite ready to do that yet.
He nodded and stepped inside behind her. Her apartment wasn't quite what he'd expected. In fact, it barely
looked as if she lived here at all. For a woman whose
workday was all about decor and color and design,
very little of that was reflected in her home. There
wasn't even so much as a colored throw rug or cush-
ion on the sofa to reflect her personality, he realized
as he looked around. No photos or anything beyond
generic art prints on the wall, either. It was about as
soulless as his hotel room.

He followed her to the kitchen.

"So? Which is it? Coffee or something stronger."

"Coffee will do, thanks."

"Black with one sugar, right?"

He nodded, surprised she'd even noticed how he
took it. Honor methodically made their coffees and
handed him his steaming mug. He wrapped his hands
around the ceramic cup, letting the warmth seep
through his skin, but it didn't touch the ice that had
taken up residence around his heart.

"Come through and sit down," she said, taking her
cup as she returned to the sitting room.

She perched on the edge of a chair, resting her elbows on her knees and holding her mug between both
hands. Logan lowered himself onto the sofa and tried
to relax. Honor's eyes still held a shocked, bruised look,
and he imagined she was reliving everything she'd
done and questioning whether she could have done
more. He knew he would, in the same situation.

"You did everything you could, Honor. Even the paramedics couldn't bring him back."

"Did I? Did I really do enough? I'll never know."

"The autopsy will give us the answers we need."

"I didn't even know he had health issues."

"Judging by the looks on Kristin's and Keaton's faces, they didn't, either. Maybe that's why he was so happy to welcome me back into the family. Maybe he knew he didn't have a lot of time left."

"Logan, I'm so sorry. You must feel dreadful. You've only just got him back and now he's gone."

Logan took a sip of his coffee and let the hot liquid burn a trail down his throat to his stomach before answering.

"They say you can't miss something you never had, but it's not true. You can." His voice broke on the last two words, and he bowed his head and closed his eyes against the stinging burn of tears.

He heard Honor's mug clunk onto the wooden coffee table, then the rustle of her clothing as she moved from her chair to the couch. She wrapped one arm around his shoulders and with her other hand she took his mug from him, set it on the table and clasped his hand.

"He was so glad you came back into his life. You can take strength from that."

"I know. I mean, I could've arrived here tomorrow instead of three weeks ago." He shook his head. "But I should've been here all my life. That's the thing that makes me the most angry at the mother who raised me. How dare she have stolen me from my true family? How dare she have kept the truth from me? If I hadn't found that box, if I'd let someone else clear the house out when she died, I might never have known any of this. I've lost two people this year. Alison Parker and Douglas Richmond—and both of them, right or wrong, were my parents."

"I can't imagine how you must be feeling right now," Honor said with genuine sympathy. "My own relationship with my mom isn't great, but I don't know how I'll react when she's gone. All I know is the person she was when I was growing up, shaped the woman I am today, for better and—" her breath hitched "—for worse. Alison Parker may have committed a terrible crime against the Richmonds and you by taking you as she did but even so, she loved you and she raised you as a good man. Your drive to succeed may not come from her, but what's in here—" She let go of his hand and tapped his chest lightly. "That's from her and the rest of the extended family you grew up as a part of. In fact, when you think about it, you're doubly lucky. You have your family in New Zealand and your family here."

"Lucky? Keaton hates me and Kristin is totally on his side. My birth mother has just lost the man she's been in love with for more than thirty-six years and barely knows me. She didn't even try to include me today—instead she reached for you." He shook his head again. "I'm an outsider here. And I'm afraid I always will be."

"Logan, no. It's still early, and you've all suffered a terrible shock. Nancy is a compassionate woman and I know she loves you—has always loved you. She'll be wondering where you are right now. It wouldn't have occurred to her to ask you to join them at the house, she would have expected it. But Keaton—" She winced. "With how he's feeling at the moment, I would guess it's best not to bait the bear in his den. I'm persona non grata, too. I feel like there's a massive void in my body. Like I don't belong anywhere, either."

"Which leaves us where?"

"Together, Logan. It leaves us together. For now, anyway."

Together sounded mighty good to him right now. More than anything else he wished they could embrace and simply find comfort in one another. He would have moved toward her, offered her comfort in his arms, but she had looked away and he could see she was struggling to hold onto her composure. As intimate as they'd been, she obviously wasn't ready to let him in and share her true emotions and, as much as that hurt him, too, he could understand it.

"We're a fine pair, aren't we?" he commented wryly.

She attempted a smile, but it was little more than a grimace. It was then that he realized she had tears slowly rolling down her cheeks. Logan pushed a strand of hair from the side of her face.

"Douglas meant a lot to you, didn't he?"

She nodded, and when she spoke her voice was thick and choked. "He taught me so much. I started at Richmond Developments straight out of college in the lowest-paid administrative role they had, and I worked my way up. He was the one who pushed me to always strive to reach further and work harder. And when he saw I was worthy, he didn't hesitate to put his weight behind me as I applied for better roles within the company.

"My dad left us when I was young. Cut off all ties to my mom and me. Douglas Richmond was more of a father figure to me than my dad ever was. I know Douglas's style didn't suit everyone, but it suited me and I owe him a lot."

"I'd say that was true of a lot of people at Richmond Developments. I didn't have the opportunity to work with him for long, but I could see how his focus brought out the best in many of the teams he had working for him."

"Keaton wouldn't agree with you there. He felt his father's methods were draconian and autocratic. They were often at loggerheads."

Logan thought about that for a moment. In the short time he'd known his brother, the only times he'd seen Keaton blow up in anger or frustration were when they were with their father. Even his anger toward Logan over Honor was a quiet seething thing. Kristin, too, had always had an air of suppressed irritation around their father at work.

"How about Kristin? She seemed really annoyed that he'd never considered her for the CEO role within the company."

"She'd make a great CEO. But that was never Douglas's plan."

"And what about you? If I'd never turned up, where would you be?"

"Where I am now, I guess, except probably still engaged to Keaton and planning a wedding."

There was a note of bitterness in her voice that he couldn't ignore.

"I'm sorry. I've really stuffed things up for you, haven't I?"

"No, I can't blame anyone but myself for where I am right now. In fact, I was in the middle of giving Douglas my notice when he collapsed." Her eyes filled with tears all over again. "I can't help but feeling that his stroke was my fault. He was arguing with me, telling me he didn't want me to leave the company."

Logan felt his gut clench in a knot at her words. She'd resigned? It was obvious that their relationship had brought her to this and knowing that filled him with frustration and regret. He hated that he'd been instrumental in making her want to leave a job that she clearly loved.

"Honor, you can't honestly believe you're responsible for him having a stroke. He was under the care of several doctors. I overheard the conversation between the police and the vascular neurologist. Douglas had been cautioned to take his condition more seriously and to make changes to his lifestyle. From what I understand, he just asked the doctor to fill his prescriptions and carried on in his inimitable way. He made his own choices, Honor. The way we all do."

She went still as she processed his words. He was surprised when she abruptly stood.

"I don't know about you, but I need something to eat. Frozen pizza and soup work for you?"

He looked at her in surprise. She wanted to eat? He suspected she just wanted to be busy, doing something that might distract her from her thoughts.

"Sure," he replied. "Let me help."

"Not much to reheating a pizza and opening a can of soup," she said dismissively.

"Hey, I've opened a lot of cans in my time. I'm expert at it," he said, rising from the sofa.

He followed her into the kitchen, where they heated the food then sat at the breakfast bar to eat it. For all her profession of hunger a few minutes ago, Honor was doing a good job of pushing her food around without eating it.

"This is going to destroy Nancy," she said abruptly. "She lived for Douglas."

"They certainly seemed close," Logan commented. "Do you think she'll keep working?"

"I don't know. Nancy is old-school. She always deferred to Douglas's wishes, barely expressed an idea of her own that he hadn't preapproved. She's going to be lost without him."

Logan considered Honor's words. It didn't sound like a terribly great way to live your life, but who was he to judge?

He wondered how Nancy was doing now, so he slid his phone from his pocket and dialed her home number before he could change his mind.

"What are you doing?" Honor asked.

"Calling to see how she is. They might have shut me out at the office, but I need my mother to know I'm thinking about her."

The phone rang several times before Keaton answered. "Richmond residence."

"Keaton, it's Logan," he said awkwardly. "I just wanted to check on you all, especially Nancy. How's she holding up?"

"As well as can be expected. Is there anything else?"

Logan tried not to be angered by his brother's tone. The man was grieving. Hell, they were all grieving.

"I would like to be there, to help support Nancy, if you'll let me," he said carefully.

"That won't be necessary. Mom's been sedated and she's in bed. Kristin and I are here."

We don't need you hung silently in the air between them. Logan had to accept what Keaton said. The last thing he wanted to do was create more strife by inserting himself into their grief.

"Okay, when she wakes, would you please pass on a message from me? Please tell her I'm thinking of her."

"Anything else?"

Logan closed his eyes and counted to three. His brother's tone was so dismissive. Could he not even put his anger with Logan over Honor aside for one moment and allow them to be brothers united in the loss of their father? It seemed not. Logan sucked in a deep breath.

"When do you expect to meet with the funeral director? I'd like to be a part of that meeting."

"I imagine that would be acceptable. He's coming to the house at ten thirty tomorrow morning. Is that all?"

Keaton obviously couldn't wait to be rid of him and, if the circumstances had been any different, Logan would have thought up something else just to tick him off in true brotherly fashion. But this was not the time.

"Thank you, no, there's nothing else. I'll see you tomorrow. And, Keaton?"

"Hmm?"

"I'm so deeply sorry for your loss."

There was silence on the other end before his brother replied.

"Yours too. See you tomorrow. Come alone."

The message was loud and clear this time. Honor was persona non grata. It was unfair. She'd been a part of the Richmond family longer than him. Before his involvement, she would have been a natural part of their family group and she deserved to be a part of it now. A fierce need to stand up for her right bloomed from deep inside him. Could he push it? Honor caught his attention and shook her head, as if she knew what he was thinking.

"Sure," he said succinctly. "See you in the morning."

Logan disconnected the call and felt his shoulders relax. At least he wasn't going to have to force his way into planning his father's farewell. But he still felt it was wrong that Honor be excluded as well. Maybe he could speak on her behalf tomorrow.

Honor looked at him as he put his phone back in his pocket.

"You okay?"

"As well as can be expected. I'm going over to the house tomorrow to meet with the funeral director."

"They don't want me there, do they?"

"I'm sorry, Honor. I'll talk to them tomorrow and—"

"No, I understand. Please don't feel bad on my account and please, don't say anything."

He saw her eyes film with tears again, but she stoically blinked them back. His being here was making things worse for her than they needed to be. Hell, his coming to Seattle had turned her life upside down. Maybe he should just go.

He pushed his plate away, all appetite now gone.

"Look, thanks for the meal. Sorry I couldn't do it justice. Let me help you clear this up and I'll be on my way."

"No need. I can do it. It's hardly a lot of cleaning up to do."

She bit her lip as if she was considering saying something else.

"What is it?" he asked.

"Nothing, I… I just wondered if you'd stay tonight. I don't really want to be alone."

Her words tumbled over one another in a rush and he couldn't help but feel a spark of relief that she still wanted him here.

"Are you sure?" he asked.

She put a hand on his arm and looked directly into his eyes.

"Please, stay. We don't have to…you know. I just think we could both benefit from the comfort of company."

"Thank you," he answered solemnly. "I'd like that."

The thought of leaving her right now was torture. She was right. They were all each other had and they needed each other right now.

They tidied the kitchen together and Honor showed him where to find the bathroom.

"There's a new toothbrush in the drawer, and you'll find fresh towels on the shelf there," she said.

When he was done, Logan walked into the bedroom and lay down on top of the covers while Honor used the bathroom. It was all so civilized, he thought. And unlike their stay in Portland, at least it wasn't fraught with the sexual tension that had driven them into one another's arms. Honor came through from the bathroom and saw Logan on top of the bed.

"You can get under the covers. I won't attack you this time."

"I know," he answered.

But even so, he remained exactly where he was.

Unable to trust himself.

Thirteen

Logan woke the next morning, curled around Honor's form beneath the sheets. Surprisingly, they'd both slept well. It felt so right to wake with her in his arms, but at the same time it brought a lot of conflicting feelings and life didn't look as though it would be getting any less complicated soon.

Honor stirred and turned to face him.

"Thank you for staying."

"It was what we both needed," he said with a smile before untangling himself from her and rising from the bed. "Don't get up. I'll let myself out."

"You don't want breakfast, or at least a coffee before you go?"

"I might get something at the hotel, but thanks. I'll see you later, okay?"

"Sure."

Back at the hotel he showered and changed, then asked the concierge for directions to a florist where he chose cut flowers for Nancy. Then he hailed a cab and headed to the Richmond home. The cab let him off outside the gates. The firmly closed gates, Logan noted as he walked toward the pillar with the intercom.

"Yes?"

Logan recognized his brother's voice immediately. "Keaton, good morning. Can you let me in?"

"You're early."

Logan bit back the response he was itching to make. Now was not the time to enter into a pissing contest with his brother.

"Yes, I am," he said quietly. "And I'd like to speak with Nancy."

There was a long pause before the gates hummed and began to smoothly open. Logan shivered in the damp, cold morning air and wished he'd thought to grab a scarf as he started down the long driveway toward the house. The gates clanged shut behind him. Keaton was waiting at the door when he reached the house.

"Nice flowers. Mom's favorites," he commented as Logan stamped his feet on the mat at the front door.

"That's just good luck," Logan admitted. "But I liked them, so it's nice to know she'll like them, too."

He looked his brother straight in the eyes. Keaton's gaze had the weary strain of someone who was still shell-shocked and yet needed to be the one everyone could turn to. More than anything, Logan wanted to share the load, but would his brother let him?

"You're looking rough, man," Logan said as he entered the house and passed Keaton the flowers so he could remove his jacket. "What can I do to help?"

Tension filled his brother's shoulders for a moment, then bit by bit, Logan saw Keaton begin to relax.

"You want to help?"

"That's what family is for, right?"

"I guess," Keaton admitted and passed the blooms back to Logan. "Mom's in the breakfast room. She's holding up pretty well today, so far at least."

"That's good to hear. And Kristin?"

"Distraught but hanging in there. She wanted to go in to the office today, but I told her we needed her here more."

"Good move. I can understand why she'd want to lose herself in work, though. It's a constant. Something you can rely on to stay mostly the same day in, day out. When you've had a big shock like this, you crave everything that's the old normal."

Keaton looked at him with a deeper understanding reflected in his gaze. "I keep forgetting you've been through this already this year. Are *you* okay?"

"I'm all right. Shocked like the rest of you. Sad I didn't have the chance to know Douglas as well as you and Kristin. I feel cheated, to be totally honest."

"Understandable. Logan, I should have included you in our family circle last night, too. It must have been shitty to have to go back to the hotel on your own."

"Actually, I stayed with Honor last night. She was pretty upset."

"Honor?" Keaton's face set in implacable lines and Logan realized that the slight softening of his brother's manner a second ago had now set into solid ice. "You know she's looking out for herself, don't you?"

"What do you mean?"

"By attaching herself to you, she's ensuring her position. I never really saw it before, but she's a corporate climber. She's solely focused on getting up that ladder, no matter what, and she'll do whatever it takes to get there."

"That's pretty harsh."

"It's the truth. You may have slept with her a couple of times, but remember I have known her for years. Looking back, I don't know why I didn't recognize it sooner. The drive that pushes her to constantly make something of herself."

Logan fought to keep the flash of anger that Keaton's words had initiated out of his voice. "Isn't that an attribute to be commended? After all, if no one wanted to better themselves, how would anyone or any corporation ever get ahead?"

"Just be wary, Logan. That's all I can say."

"With all due respect, I think you've got her wrong. Whatever bitterness you may feel over what happened the night I arrived in Seattle—and yes, you're entitled to that bitterness—it's misplaced. She thought I was you."

"And when she knew you weren't? In Portland?"

"Yeah, well in that instance, we were equally to

blame. Look, I know you, and we might never be as close as we could have been if we'd been raised together, but I really want to apologize for allowing Honor to become a wedge between us."

"And yet you spent last night with her?" Keaton looked at him incredulously.

"She needed someone. She watched our father die right in front of her and she worked damn hard to try to bring him back. You know why she was in his office, don't you?"

"I assume she was having a meeting with him."

"She was. To give him her resignation."

"What?" Keaton sounded shocked.

"And you want to know why?"

"I'm sure you're about to tell me."

"Because she felt guilty about what she'd done and how it was making it impossible for *us* to get along. Does that sound like the kind of thing a corporate climber would do?"

Logan heard light footsteps on the parquet flooring, and Nancy came into the front entrance.

"Keaton? Who's at the do—" She stopped in her tracks when she saw the two men standing together in the foyer. "Oh, Logan, you've come. I'm so glad."

"Nancy, I brought you these," Logan said, stepping toward his mother and offering her the flowers.

She ignored them at first and stepped in close to give him a hug. "Thank you. It wasn't right not having you here last night. I need you all more than you could ever know. We need each other at this horrible, horrible time."

In her tight embrace, Logan had to fight back the sting of tears. He swallowed against the emotion that swelled up from deep inside him, choking him. She had no idea how much he needed them, too.

In typical motherly fashion, Nancy asked, "Have you eaten yet? Come through to the breakfast room. Our housekeeper does great French toast, and now that you're here I feel a little appetite returning. Are you coming, Keaton?"

She took the flowers from Logan, making approving noises over the blooms, and headed toward the back of the house. Logan and Keaton made eye contact.

"We'll continue our discussion another time," Keaton said.

"Yes, we most definitely will," Logan answered.

The rest of the week passed in a blur with Christmas Day being the quietest Logan had ever known as they waited and prepared for Douglas's funeral. At Nancy's request, he'd moved out of the hotel and into a guest suite at her home. With Kristin and Keaton in their own places, Logan felt it was the least he could do to support his mom. She'd also asked that he call her Mom, and while it had felt a little awkward to begin with, now it felt right.

Unfortunately, at the same time, that discussion with Keaton never stood a chance of happening, and the tension that simmered between the brothers only seemed to get stronger. And, at the office, Honor seemed hell bent on keeping clear of him on the few times he'd called in. She'd avoided his phone calls to check in on her, too. She was never far from his thoughts and it worried him, wondering how she was coping.

On the morning of the funeral, the siblings met with Nancy in the foyer of the house as the driver and car from the funeral home pulled up to take them to the service. Logan had finally managed to get hold of Honor and offered her a ride to the cemetery, but she'd said she'd make her own way. Nancy, who'd been stoic and surprisingly strong in the preceding days, today appeared fragile and absolutely lost. Douglas's wish had been for a short graveside service only, and despite the frigid weather they'd agreed to observe his request. Even so, Nancy had insisted on a catered gathering at the house immediately afterward for all those who'd wanted to pay their respects and remember him.

When the car pulled up at the cemetery, Logan felt as if a giant weight had settled in his chest. The four of them, dressed in heavy coats, hats, scarves and gloves, made their way toward the people who were already assembling at the graveside. Puffs of air filled the spaces between them all as people talked and milled about in small groups, the sea of bodies separating slightly as Nancy and her children joined the throng.

Logan's eyes searched out Honor, who excused herself from a group she was talking with and walked over to Nancy, giving the woman a huge hug and sharing some quiet words. Nancy clung to her a moment before reaching in her pocket for a tissue.

"You'll sit with us, won't you? And you'll come back to the house, too?" Nancy said. "I know you and

Keaton aren't engaged anymore, but I feel like you're one of my own and I know Douglas felt the same."

Honor's eyes flicked to Keaton for a moment. Whatever she saw reflected in his face made her shoulders relax a little as she nodded and smiled back at Nancy.

"If everyone else is okay with that?"

Honor looked from Keaton to Kristin and finally to Logan. He stared back at her, taking in the shadows beneath her eyes and the slight frown on her forehead. He wanted nothing more than to gather her in his arms and offer her comfort, as Nancy had done, but she took a step back.

"You can sit by me," he offered when his siblings remained silent.

"Thank you," she said on a tightly issued breath. It was almost time for the service to begin when a last-minute group consisting of two men and two women, related judging by their resemblance to each other, arrived and made their way toward the graveside.

"Do you know them?" Logan asked his sister.

"Never seen them before," she replied. "Maybe they're business associates of Dad's."

To Logan's surprise, they assumed seats in the first row in front of the waiting casket. Seats that had been reserved for Nancy, Keaton, Kristin and Logan. The eldest woman, in her fifties by the look of her, appeared quiet and composed but pale. Her children, too, had similar expressions, and Logan couldn't help but feel there was something familiar about them. He watched as the funeral director approached them.

"Excuse me, ma'am. Could you move to the next row

back, please? These seats are reserved for the widow and children of Mr. Richmond," Logan heard the man say discreetly.

They were all surprised when the woman vehemently shook her head.

"Ma'am, please," the funeral director urged again, a little less gently this time.

Logan stepped up to the newcomers and put a hand on the funeral director's shoulder.

"Let me," he said firmly before turning to the newcomers. "Perhaps you could move back a row, please? These seats were reserved for my family."

The woman looked at him, and for a moment her eyes blazed with suppressed fury.

"*Your* family? I have *every* right to be at the graveside of my husband's burial and so do our children!"

"Logan?" Nancy drew closer. "What is that woman saying?"

The woman in question stood, her children following suit, almost as if they formed an honor guard flanking her. Nancy's children did the same.

"I'm saying I have every right to be right here," the other woman shouted as she pointed to the seat she'd just vacated. "I am Douglas Richmond's wife and I can prove it."

"Ma'am… Mrs. Richmond, perhaps now is not the time." The funeral director tried to insert himself between the families.

"Really?" said the second Mrs. Richmond. "If not now, when? My husband has died and this woman has organized his burial without my permission."

She turned to face Nancy, who looked incapable of speech. "I was prepared to let this go, to let you go ahead and bury my husband before stating my claim, but now I'm not feeling so inclined. In fact, I want Douglas's body brought back to Virginia where he belongs."

"What are you talking about? He's my husband and he's being buried in accordance with his wishes." Nancy's voice shook with the emotion evident in her strained features.

"Well, they're not my wishes and as his wife, I'm telling you this is not going ahead."

"I'm his wife," Nancy countered.

Logan looked from one woman to the next and back again as their voices rose in anger. Then Keaton and Kristin entered the fray together with the other Mrs. Richmond's children. This had to stop before it became some sordid story in the news. Logan tugged on the funeral director's arm. The poor man looked as though he was paralyzed in shock.

"Obviously this can't go ahead until we've sorted this mess out," Logan said firmly. "Let's clear everyone away and take this elsewhere."

The man looked relieved to be given a clear instruction, and he and his staff moved to shepherd the gathered mourners well away from the verbal fracas taking place at the graveside. Logan stepped back up to the melee and held up a hand.

"People, can we please stop for a minute. Obviously, there is some discussion to be had and proof to be given before we can go any further. Might I suggest we take this back to the house?" he said in a voice that brooked no discussion.

"Good idea," said Keaton. "This is preposterous. This woman is saying she and Dad were married two years before him and Mom. It can't be true. That would make him a bigamist."

The daughter of the other Mrs. Richmond cast a scornful glance at the highly polished, flower-bedecked coffin poised over the grave. "If the shoe fits," she said succinctly.

Nancy and Kristin both looked as though they were about to launch themselves at her. Honor, who'd been standing nearby, stepped between them. Grateful to avoid a full-on physical confrontation, Logan suggested everyone get back to their cars and reconvene at Nancy's house.

"I'm not setting foot inside that woman's house," the other Mrs. Richmond stated firmly.

"Then perhaps you'd prefer to leave and allow us to continue with my father's farewell," Logan said darkly, his eyes flicking from her to her children and back again.

"I most certainly would not," she spluttered indignantly.

"Then I would respectfully ask you to put your emotions aside for a few hours while we discuss this in a reasonable and rational way," Logan suggested. "Mom? Are you okay with that?"

Nancy wavered slightly where she stood, prompting Kristin to take her arm to steady her.

"I don't understand this, but I guess it will be okay.

Where's Hector?" Nancy asked, scanning the crowd for the family's lawyer. "I saw him here before. He should be there, too, shouldn't he?"

She looked to Logan, who nodded and said, "Yes, he should."

"He's heading to his car," Honor said. "I'll go stop him."

Logan murmured his thanks and watched as she briskly walked toward the roadside, where groups of people continued to linger despite being asked to move on. He saw Honor catch up with Hector Ramirez and watched as the two of them spoke before Hector nodded and waited by his car. Gratitude mixed with pride for her filled him—even given how she was being treated by Keaton and Kristin, she was willing to step up and help.

"I'll speak with him now if we're all agreed?" Logan asked.

He looked at each person in turn, not moving onto the next until they'd all nodded their consent. The funeral director scurried toward them.

"I've never had this happen in forty years of business. What am I to do with Mr. Richmond?" he asked.

"Perhaps you could take him back to the funeral home until we clear this up."

"Yes, yes. That's what I'll do."

Muttering to himself, the man gestured to his staff, and they began to assemble their equipment to return the coffin to the hearse parked by the curb. Turning his back to the activity, Logan followed his family, and the other family, back to the waiting cars by the sidewalk. He gave Nancy's address to the driver who'd brought the other family and suggested the man follow behind Nancy's car.

"Look after Mom," Logan directed Keaton and Kristin, who appeared to be equal parts stricken and furious right now. "And don't allow any discussion until I get there with Hector."

"You're coming with him?"

"I am."

"And Honor?"

"I think Nancy would want her there. Besides, you'll need someone to deal with the caterers and staff while we're all dealing with that lot," Logan said firmly. He wasn't about to cut Honor out now.

To his relief Keaton nodded. "Okay. We'll see you back at the house. Thanks for stepping up and taking charge there."

"Hey, what else is a big brother for?" Logan said in an attempt to defuse the tension that now gripped everyone.

Keaton snorted a laugh. "You're not so big I couldn't take you."

Logan smiled back, feeling something ease deep within his chest. They might not be the perfect family and he might not be close to his siblings, but he had the feeling that right now they needed him more than they'd ever dreamed possible—and he would be there for them, one hundred percent.

Fourteen

Hector and Logan spoke in undertones up front as Hector drove them to the Richmond family home. Honor listened but didn't contribute to the conversation. In fact, she had no idea what to say or think about any of this aside from agreeing it was almost farcical to have a whole other family arrive at Douglas's funeral claiming to be his.

She looked out the window and tried to figure out how Douglas could have possibly maintained two completely separate lives and families for so long without being caught. Why on earth would a man do something like that? Surely he knew that eventually his deceit would be discovered. Was that what he'd been talking about the day he died when he mentioned people making mistakes—some more than others? Had he been thinking of his own decisions? Either way, if these people's claims were true, what he'd done was immoral, not to mention illegal.

And speaking about the legality of it, where did this leave everyone in terms of succession at Richmond Developments? Had Logan and Keaton even thought about that yet? Douglas had never made any secret of the fact that his firstborn heir would be appointed to head up the company on his death. What if his son from his first wife was older than Logan and Keaton? And were Logan, Keaton and Kristin now illegitimate?

Her mind spun on the possibilities until she felt dizzy. One thing was absolutely certain, however, and that was the effect this betrayal by their father would have on his children. All of them. Honor knew a lot about betrayal. The scars ran deep and had lifelong ramifications. From what Honor could tell, for all their privilege, Kristin and Keaton had spent their whole lives trying to please their father. Finding out he might have had another family had to be doing a number on both of them.

She looked at the back of Logan's head and wondered how he felt about it all. He had barely had a chance to get to know Douglas, so was he even surprised about today's events? He certainly had stepped up and taken control pretty quickly. Even Keaton hadn't pushed back when Logan had done that. She was relieved to see the brothers working together and it firmed her resolve to create as much distance between herself and Logan as she possibly could. He deserved his family, unfettered by the complications she brought to everything, no matter how deeply she felt for him.

The lawyer pulled into the driveway at the Richmond house and parked outside the front door. They alighted and the men went inside, but Honor paused to ensure the gate at the end of the driveway was closed first. The last thing they needed now was rubberneckers joining the party; she had no doubt that the gossip mill was already churning away over what had happened at the graveside. She then went out to the kitchen and advised the caterers to contact a local homeless shelter to see if they'd accept the food that had been prepared for the guests who would now no longer be coming. She suggested to Nancy's housekeeper that she keep some platters aside for the family, who were now assembled in the parlor at the front of the house.

When she joined the family in the formal parlor, you could just about cut the seething, silent atmosphere with a knife. Her eyes sought out Logan, who remained standing as everyone else took their seats. The families lined up facing one another on Nancy's favorite chairs, all bearing very similar expressions. This wasn't going to be pleasant but she felt a swell of respect for Logan, who looked as if he'd more than capably chair this awkward meeting. Her instincts urged her to stand by him and offer him the support he was due but she knew she couldn't, and that just about crushed the air from her lungs. She'd thought she would cope with being near him again today, but it was proving more difficult than she'd imagined. Even so, she couldn't just desert him, or Nancy for that matter. Not when they might need her help.

"I think we can agree that today's developments have come as a shock," Logan started.

"I am not a development," the other Mrs. Richmond stated firmly. "I am Douglas's first and legal wife. She and her spawn are the *development*, and a very unwelcome one, I can tell you."

"Mom, don't. We are all shocked. There's no need to be unkind. None of this is anyone's fault except for Dad's," her daughter said firmly.

"You're right," Logan said in agreement. "First, I think we need to introduce ourselves, then, if you have no objections, we can ask Hector for his legal opinion on the situation."

The woman snorted. "As if his opinion will be unbiased. You can rest assured, my lawyers will be all over this no matter what your man says."

Logan said nothing but fixed his gaze on her and raised a brow.

"Fine," she said on another outraged huff of breath. "My name is Eleanor Richmond. I married Douglas on the first of July, thirty-six years ago, in our hometown in Virginia. We were high school sweethearts. These are our children—Fletcher, Mathias and Lisa."

"And I am Nancy Richmond. I, too, married Douglas thirty-six years ago, on the second of September, here in Seattle. We had a whirlwind courtship. He told me he couldn't live without me and begged me to marry him. And these are my children—Logan, Keaton and Kristin."

"And this is Hector Ramirez, our family lawyer," Logan introduced the attorney, who was sitting quietly to one side of the room observing the proceedings. "Hector, would you like to say a few words?"

"Thank you, Logan. I knew Douglas for many years, and I have to say this development has shocked me as much as it has clearly shocked you all. The first step I believe we need to take is to ascertain whose marriage has legal standing. Once that is done, the way forward will be clearer."

"The way forward?" Nancy asked.

"In terms of the execution of Douglas's final wishes. Aside from his personal effects, which he has been quite explicit in naming the recipients of, there's the matter of his business."

"My husband maintained a well-respected construction company in Virginia," Eleanor interjected. "Don't for one minute think that her children will be entitled to any of that or my home or financial portfolios."

Honor watched as Hector blinked in surprise at the barely suppressed vitriol in the other woman's voice. She herself was shocked, too. The woman hardly acted like a grieving widow. More like an avenging one. Her son Fletcher leaned forward and began to speak.

"Mom, this is going to be complicated enough as it is without you stirring the pot. If you have nothing positive to add, then, under the circumstances, it would be best if you kept your thoughts to yourself."

"Fletcher, that's unfair. I am your father's legal widow. You are his legitimate children. I'm making a stand for what's ours. For what's right."

"Then let's allow the lawyers to determine this quickly. The longer we take over this, the longer both our businesses and all our lives will be in limbo." Fletcher looked up at everyone assembled. "Are we agreed on that?"

There were murmurs of assent all round.

Fletcher slid out a business card and passed it to Hector. "If you could let us know exactly what you need from us to prove my mother's claim, we will advise our lawyers to provide that information accordingly. We will be staying in town tonight before flying back home tomorrow."

"And we'll be demanding that Douglas's body be returned to Virginia when this is all settled," Eleanor snapped at Nancy.

Honor couldn't believe the other woman's unpleasant attitude. Nancy had done no wrong. To her credit, Nancy didn't lower herself to respond; she merely turned to Hector and thanked him before proving herself the consummate hostess by offering everyone assembled something to eat and drink. Eleanor's second son, Mathias, refused on behalf of his family.

"If you don't mind, we'll make our way back to the hotel. I think you'll agree this is hardly a social situation that we'd like to prolong."

"Of course," Keaton said, standing and offering his hand to each of his purported half brothers and sister. "We all have a lot to process."

"You can say that again," Kristin muttered as she rose to her feet as well.

Eleanor merely sniffed as she stood up and led the

way to the front door, her children following behind. Honor moved quickly to open the door and show them out. Eleanor didn't even acknowledge her, but Lisa smiled her thanks as she walked past. Once they were settled in their car, Honor activated the gate and waited until she caught the flicker of taillights at the end of the driveway before closing it again. Only then did she begin to feel her body start to relax.

"We sure weren't expecting that," Logan said from behind her.

She turned around slowly, forcing herself to ignore the way her heartrate kicked up a beat at his nearness. "No, we certainly weren't. Don't you think it odd that Douglas maintained mirror lives on each side of the country? If what they're saying is true."

"Odd isn't the word I'd choose." Logan wiped a hand across his face. "What a mess."

Her heart ached for him. Now that the confrontation was over, for now at least, the strain Logan was feeling was clear on his face. Honor hastened to choose words that might be of some encouragement.

"I can't help but feel that something isn't right about it all. Eleanor was so…aggressive, for want of a better word. It almost made me feel as if she was hiding something."

"You got that, too, huh?"

Honor sighed and reminded herself that while they were on the same wavelength, she could offer him no more than words right now. "This situation is going to make a whole bunch of lawyers very rich, isn't it?"

"Yeah," he agreed, his expression grim. "We're

all going to be on tenterhooks until we know exactly where we stand."

Honor nodded. "Look, you all have a lot to discuss. I'll call a cab and head off and leave you to your privacy."

"Are you sure you won't stay? Nancy wouldn't object."

And you? she wanted to ask even though she knew the answer. It was clear in his expression that he was torn. She knew he wanted to include her, but was mindful of what her presence would do to his siblings. No, it was better she went, no matter how much it tore her apart to leave him at a time like this.

"I know," she said softly. "But it's better this way. Trust me."

He took her hand and she instantly felt awareness tingle through her at his touch.

"Thank you for all you've done today. I mean it. You gave me strength when I needed it."

Her throat choked on all the words she wished she could say in reply. She swallowed hard and said, "Give Nancy my regards."

Then she let herself out the door and closed it firmly behind her.

Fifteen

Two weeks later and they were no closer to a resolution. And, worse, Douglas continued to remain unburied, which was a deep source of distress to Nancy. Hector had advised the family that, based on the information provided by Eleanor's lawyer, including notarized copies of documents, her marriage to Douglas had indeed taken place prior to Nancy's, which made Nancy's claim the invalid one. The shame and sorrow at discovering she'd been deceived for so long had had a huge impact on her health, and she'd been unable to work since Douglas's death.

"How was Mom this morning?" Kristin asked as she popped into the office that had been her dad's and which was now, temporarily at least, Logan's.

"Still the same. I can't seem to get her interested in anything, and believe me, I've tried."

"Yeah, Keaton said she won't even leave the house. She's terrified she'll bump into someone she knows and she can't stand to face the questions, or worse, the pity."

The only bright side of this whole debacle was that it had drawn the siblings closer together. Not only were they dedicated to providing a united front of support to their mom, but also to the staff. So far, they'd managed to continue with business as usual and the three had worked together on major decisions and planning.

Honor had insisted she was working out the notice she'd given to Douglas on the day he died and had proven intractable on the subject. Not even a plea from Keaton had swayed her. And she'd gone back to avoiding Logan as much as possible. When they did cross paths, she kept herself apart and kept their conversations short. It was driving him crazy.

Logan leaned back in his chair and swiveled it around to look out the window. He still couldn't believe his father had managed to maintain two families for most of his life without anyone discovering his deception until now. What kind of man did that?

"You okay?" Kristin asked as she moved over toward the window and stared out at the view with him.

"I guess. I just can't get my head around what he did and how he did it."

Kristin shook her head. "I know what you mean. To us, he and Mom were always a tight unit. Totally devoted to one another. Yes, he traveled a lot with work, but no one would have suspected that he lived a double life. I feel so betrayed—I can't even begin to imagine how this is messing with Mom. He was her entire life and that life was a complete and utter lie."

"Not a complete lie," Logan said, trying to reassure her. "He loved Nancy deeply. Anyone could see that."

"But he loved Eleanor, too. And how he could love that woman is totally beyond me."

"I think it's probably fair to say we didn't see her at her best."

Kristin snorted. "That's true. How did she find out about Dad's death, anyway? Why didn't she or her lawyers make contact before the funeral?"

Logan sighed. "From what I have gleaned from Fletcher, she saw the notice in the paper and pretty much ordered the kids to book the flights and come with her. I'm not sure she had a plan—she just wanted to stake her claim."

"Well, she certainly did that. And how're things with our big brother from the East Coast? Is he champing at the bit to take over here?"

"For now he's like us. Waiting for the appropriate confirmation before any further decisions are made. In the meantime, he's focusing on business over there, and we need to keep doing what we do here."

"I hate waiting."

"We're agreed on that one. Keaton's frustrated, too."

"And Honor? She's still adamant she's leaving?"

Logan felt that all-too-familiar twist in his chest when he heard her name. They'd barely seen one another. She'd been busy ensuring her work was fully up-to-date and ready to hand over to her replacement as well as training her assistant and his colleagues on holding the reins in her department until an appointment was made. On top of that, she'd sent her assistant to attend any department meetings in her stead.

"Yeah," he answered dully.

He really missed her. Not just physically, but he missed her quick wit, her intelligent observations about work—everything. He kept telling himself it was ridiculous. They'd only met at the beginning of December and here they were, halfway into January and he couldn't get her to budge from his mind. Even in sleep she invaded his dreams, making him wake aching and frustrated and wishing she was there. He'd never experienced anything like it before.

"You know, I think Keaton would be okay now if you and Honor—" Kristin started.

"No. I can't go there."

"But, seriously. He isn't acting like a spurned lovelorn idiot. If you ask me, he got over her far more quickly than a man engaged to a woman should. Dad always said they were a good match but not a perfect one."

"Like he was an expert on relationships," Logan commented wryly.

"Yeah," Kristin laughed. "You're probably right. But it's a shame. Honor is a really awesome person. We've all enjoyed her friendship and her talents here at the office."

"Has HR advertised her position yet?"

"Yes, and they've had applicants, but none of them are of her caliber."

Logan closed his eyes briefly. And that was the problem, he thought. No one else was Honor Gould. And no one else had ever affected him quite as deeply as she had, either.

Honor couldn't help it. Waiting around had never been a particularly strong suit of hers, and the suspense surrounding the Richmond family situation was beginning to take its toll on everyone around her. Several of her team had expressed concern at the stability of the company with no officially appointed CEO, while others were more concerned about the idea of a total stranger coming from the East Coast to run the place. One or two had even handed in their notice already. While Honor had done her best to try and dissuade them, with her own last day fast approaching, no matter how she phrased things, it came across as hypocritical to try to talk people into staying.

On the few occasions her path had crossed with the Richmond siblings, she'd seen the obvious strain on their faces, and it upset her that Nancy had yet to return to work. She understood they were all grieving, but the complexity of Douglas's family relationships had created an added burden. The only bright side to any of this was seeing how Logan, Keaton and Kristin had begun to work together as a tight unit. And that made her choice to go worthwhile.

She loved Logan. And loving him meant she was prepared to do whatever it took to ensure he was happy. She understood his need for family, for identity, and she respected that was paramount for him right now.

She was the last person who'd expect him to give up everything he'd just gotten back for her. And she knew that it would be a her-or-them situation. That much had been made clear when Kristin, who'd been her closest female confidante, had closed ranks with Keaton against her.

There had to be something she could do to make things right for them before she left. She'd thought long and hard about the whole situation with Douglas's second family, and no matter how she'd looked at it, it simply didn't feel right with her. There'd been something about Eleanor's behavior—not merely defensive, but aggressive—that made Honor want to look deeper into her claims. Yes, she knew that Hector Ramirez had received the information that Eleanor's lawyers had sent through. On the surface everything appeared to be legitimate, so far. But a feeling still niggled at Honor that she was missing something.

Growing up where Honor had, she'd seen and studied at close quarters what happened when people got caught in a lie, and in her experience, they behaved in one of three ways—they capitulated and admitted guilt, they acted like it didn't matter, or they went head-on at the challenge and their aggression would make the other person back off. Her gut told her that Eleanor's behavior fell into the latter category.

Judging by the information provided by Eleanor so far, she and Douglas were married on July first, as she'd said. Fletcher's birth had come seven months later, so Honor was pretty sure that Eleanor had been expecting him already when she and Douglas had mar-

ried. Not that there was any scandal to that even if
they'd just been fresh out of high school. And Fletcher's
date of birth definitely made him around eighteen
months older than Logan and Keaton, which threw
Douglas's succession plans for Richmond Developments well and truly into the fire.

Not for the first time, Honor wondered what the
heck he'd been thinking. Surely he'd known that when
he died his sordid truths would come creeping out of
the woodwork, hadn't he? Had he had such a God complex that he thought he'd be able to keep all his plates
spinning and that no one would ever discover the truth?
Had he no idea how hurtful and cruel his choices had
been?

Honor reached her decision. Even if it meant she
had to eat canned soup for the rest of the month, she
was going to hire a private investigator to dig up the
dirt she just knew to the soles of her feet hung around
Douglas and Eleanor's marriage. She owed it to the
Richmonds. To Douglas for always encouraging her,
to Keaton to right the wrongs she'd done him and to
Logan especially because after all he'd been through
he deserved the very best. She might have jeopardized
his position in his family, but if she could help to put
things right, she would.

A week later she received the report from the
Norfolk-based investigator she'd hired. The woman had
set out the information she'd gleaned with crisp clar-
ity and as Honor read through the data, she began to
wonder if she'd been wasting both her time and money.

Until she reached the last couple of pages, whereupon she felt a sudden spike in adrenaline and a tremor of excitement shook her body. Without waiting another moment, she grabbed the report and headed for Douglas's office.

"Stella, is Logan in?" she asked the assistant as she all but skidded to a halt on the carpet.

"He is, but he's in a meeting with Keaton, Kristin and Hector Ramirez right now."

"That's good. I need to see them, too."

Without waiting for Stella to announce her, she pushed open the office door and walked straight in. All four heads swiveled to see who had interrupted and Stella followed hard on Honor's heels, muttering apologies for the intrusion.

"That's okay, Stella. Obviously it's important. Perhaps you could organize someone to bring some coffee in for us?" Logan said.

"Certainly. It will be here right away."

Honor waited for Stella to close the door behind her before speaking.

"Look, I'm sorry to barge in on you all like this, but I just found out something really important and you need to know."

"What kind of important?" Kristin asked.

"Important to all of you, and your half brothers and sister. But most of all, it's going to be very important to Nancy."

"Well, spit it out," Keaton said impatiently.

"Hang on. First of all, take a seat, Honor," Logan

suggested and gestured to the only vacant seat in the office, right in front of him.

Honor sat down but could still feel the tension that had driven her to the office in such a hurry holding her in its grip. Logan reached for the water carafe on the tray on his desk and poured her a glass of water and pushed it in her direction.

"Here, you look like you could do with this," he said.

"Thanks," she said with a grateful smile.

Her hand shook slightly as she lifted the glass to her lips and drank half of it in one gulp.

"Right, would you like to share your information with us?" Logan prodded gently.

"From the beginning I felt like there was something not quite right about Eleanor's claim. I had a feeling she was trying to hide the full truth."

"What's she trying to hide? Everything Hector has presented to us here today stacks up as the truth," Keaton said in a tone that would have stopped her under any other circumstances.

"That's what she wants you to see. But what she doesn't want you to see is this." Honor put the report from her investigator on the desk in front of them. She flipped through to the last page and stabbed at it with her finger. "This is what Eleanor didn't want anyone to know. She was underage when she and Douglas married."

Hector leaned forward and read the document. "Yes, that's true. But in the state of Virginia if you're under the age of eighteen and have the permission of your parents, you can legally marry."

"Yes, but Eleanor didn't have her parents' permission," Honor insisted.

"According to the data we've gleaned from the circuit court clerk, she did. It states her mother signed the necessary permissions."

Honor shook her head vehemently. "But her mother couldn't have done that. She was in Monte Carlo at the time, with her husband, Eleanor's father. They were on a six-month tour of Europe. Neither of them could have given permission because they weren't there when the license application was completed."

"So you're saying the license is invalid?" Kristin said, leaning forward in excitement.

Honor nodded and waited for Hector to finish reading the report summary she'd put in front of them.

"So it would seem," he said in agreement. "According to this report, Eleanor bribed her parents' housekeeper to pretend to be her mother when the application was made for the license. A handwriting expert has verified that the signature on the application is not the same as that on record for Eleanor's mother."

"Why would she do such a thing?" Keaton asked, looking totally stunned by the revelation.

"I don't know for sure, but from what the investigator was able to find out, Honor was only seventeen when she found out she was pregnant with Fletcher. The housekeeper has since passed away, but the investigator talked to her daughter. Apparently the poor woman lived her life in fear of being found out for impersonating her boss. She had a habit of helping herself to Eleanor's father's good brandy. Eleanor knew this and threatened to tell her father if the housekeeper didn't help Eleanor with her plan to marry Douglas before her parents returned from Europe.

"Eleanor believed that if she was already married to Douglas, her parents couldn't do anything about it, and since she was pregnant they'd have to accept Douglas, too. Seems they'd had greater aspirations for their daughter up until then, which included a Swiss finishing school and the likelihood of a marriage to the son of a family friend, who was a diplomat."

"Wow, you kind of have to feel sorry for her. She must have been terribly desperate to go to those lengths," Kristin said with a liberal dose of sympathy.

"According to the housekeeper's daughter, Eleanor's parents disowned her on their return from Europe. Her father was a high-ranking naval officer and her mother was from a very wealthy family. On their deaths, their entire estate went to a naval charity. Eleanor got nothing."

"And from the looks of her claim on Dad's estate, she's still trying to make up for that," Keaton said.

Hector cleared his throat noisily before speaking. "I think the key thing here is that Douglas and Nancy's marriage is the one that's valid."

"Which means that Logan is Dad's chosen CEO for Richmond Developments," Kristin added.

"Yes, and that woman and her children have no claim on our company," Keaton said vehemently.

Logan leaned back in his chair, and Honor was relieved to see the lines of tension that had scored his face over these past few weeks begin to ease.

"So, it's business as usual?" he asked Hector directly.

"I believe so. I'll head back to my office and prepare a letter for Eleanor Richmond's lawyers requesting that she drop all claims to Douglas's body, and to his business interests here on the West Coast based on the information that Ms. Gould has brought to us. They will no doubt need to verify the information uncovered in the private investigator's report. The question now arises as to whether you wish to state a claim on your father's business interests in Virginia."

"We could do that?" Keaton asked.

Hector shrugged slightly. "Under the terms of your father's will, you probably could."

"But more important is, would we want to," Logan said, playing devil's advocate. "Do we really want to subject Fletcher, Mathias and Lisa to what we've been going through?"

"Absolutely not," Keaton said vehemently. "When all's said and done, we're all family, whether we like it or not."

Honor watched as Logan looked to his sister.

"I don't see why we should allow Dad's actions to victimize us any further, do you?" she asked.

"Then we three are agreed," he said and directed his attention back to Hector. "Please make it clear to Eleanor and her family that, provided she drops her claims, we will not make any counterclaims against our father's interests in Virginia. Also inform her that we will proceed with honoring our father's wishes regarding his interment here in Seattle."

They all stood, and Hector shook hands with each of the siblings before turning to Honor. "I trust that I can take this copy of the report?"

"Of course," she said fervently.

Hector nodded and made his goodbyes. Once he was gone, Logan looked at Honor.

"Thank you," he said, his voice laden with relief. "Without your hard work things could have turned out very different, for all of us. We owe you for that."

Honor met his gaze and her voice shook as she answered him. "No, I owed you all. I had to do something."

Logan looked as if he wanted to object but she shook her head slightly and he got the message. He turned to his brother and sister.

"So, now we know this is ours, are you two ready to help me run it?"

"Aren't we doing that already?" Kristin asked.

"Not the way I was thinking," Logan continued. "How about we take a good hard look at the company structure? I think it's time we assumed joint control of Richmond Developments."

"Are you serious? How on earth will that work?" Keaton asked skeptically.

Logan shrugged. "We'll figure it out, but most importantly, are you guys on board?"

Both Keaton and Kristin nodded.

"I think we should head over to Mom's and let her know the news face-to-face. What do you think?" Keaton said.

"That's a great idea," Kristin said. "Are you coming, too, Honor? After all, if not for your hard work, we'd still be waiting for the next ax to fall."

Honor smiled and shook her head. "No, I need to finalize a few things here this afternoon, but I have to say I'm really glad you guys will be working together. I'm sure you'll have your differences—you're all such strong-minded individuals—but if you could pull together the way you have since Douglas died, I'm sure you can work through anything. Good luck."

"Are you sure, Honor? You could come later," Kristin pressed.

"No, really. I'm really busy, and this is a special time for you all as a family," Honor insisted.

"Are you coming with us now, Logan?" Keaton asked.

"I just want to say a few words to Honor first. You guys go ahead. I'll be there soon."

After they'd gone, Logan looked at Honor. She ached to move forward into his arms. To lay her head on his chest and feel his warmth and hear the strength of his heartbeat. To maybe lift her face to his and kiss him, even if it was just one last time. Because she'd reached a decision today. After delivering the information from the private investigator to the family, she planned to leave, immediately. Staying here was slowly tearing her apart. They might not give her a reference for not working out her full two weeks, but she didn't care anymore. She just needed to remove herself from a situation that was becoming more painful every day.

She fought back the urge to cry and lifted her chin

slightly as she asked, "What was it you wanted to talk to me about?"

"I can't begin to tell you how much I appreciate you bringing that information to us."

"I had to. I owe all of you—your parents, too."

"You don't owe me anything," Logan said.

"Maybe not now, but I did. I nearly ruined your chance to build the family you always wanted. I hope we're clear now."

"Hardly. We all owe you."

She shook her head. "No, it's my gift to you."

She started to leave.

"Honor, wait. Don't go. Please. Let's work this out."

"We can't work it out, Logan. Every time I'm in the same space as you and Keaton I'm driving a wedge between you. I won't do that to you. You deserve so much more than that."

And then, using every ounce of control she had in her, she turned on her heels and walked out of his office and out of his life, forever.

Sixteen

The biting cold of January had eased up in February, but it was still darned cold. Back in New Zealand, temperatures were at sweltering levels with hot, sticky nights and high levels of humidity. Logan had Skyped with his grandmother, whose fluffy white hair had been blown sideways by the large fan oscillating next to her. He'd offered to put air-conditioning in her house on more than one occasion, but she'd insisted she was fine. He missed her. He missed all of them, and he'd scheduled a trip home in April.

But there was one person he missed more than everyone else altogether.

Honor.

He'd been shocked when he'd discovered she'd cleared out her office after delivering the report that had seen Eleanor Richmond pull back on her claims against Douglas's estate. Fletcher, Mathias and Lisa had traveled to Douglas's interment ceremony, and all six of his children were working toward establishing a stronger connection. So, instead of discovering his lost family, Logan had discovered two. But that side of things apart, there was still a yawning hole in Logan's life where Honor belonged.

"You're daydreaming again, Logan," Keaton said from across the meeting room table. "Care to share your thoughts?"

The two men had been discussing their roles and responsibilities under the new regime that had been approved by the board. And so far at least, there'd been no head-to-head disagreements.

"Sorry, Keaton. Look, maybe we can take a break for ten minutes."

Keaton pushed his chair back from the table. "Good idea. Let's go grab a coffee at the place downstairs. We could both do with the change in scenery."

After ordering their identical coffees, one of many things they'd discovered they had in common, Keaton led the way to a small table by the window. Once they were seated, he pinned Logan with a stare.

"What?" Logan said. "You're starting to creep me out, brother."

"Something's wrong. You're different."

"I thought we were still getting to know one another. How can I be different?"

Keaton shook his head. "No, don't try to hedge with me. You're as on point in the office as you've been right from the start, but something's missing inside you. It's Honor, isn't it?"

Logan felt his defenses shoot up. "I'm not seeing her, if that's what you're getting at."

The girl at the counter called out his name, and he rose to collect their order before sitting back down again.

"Actually, no. That wasn't what I was getting at," Keaton said as they put sugar in their black coffees and stirred in synchronization. "Do you love her?"

"Keaton, don't do this. You know I wouldn't do anything to destroy our relationship as brothers."

The bond between them was growing stronger but Logan doubted that it would survive him striking up again with Keaton's ex-fiancée. That definitely went against the guy code, and he'd already overstepped that mark. As much as he wanted to, he wasn't about to put his feelings for Honor ahead of the fragile bond that was growing between him and Keaton.

"We're doing okay," Keaton admitted. "I have to say I didn't want to like you, but I do. Although it still feels weird seeing myself every time I look at you."

"Same." Logan took a sip of his coffee. "Shall we head back and finish our business?"

"Hang on. I'm not done. I'm worried about you."

Logan spread his hands and shrugged. "Nothing to worry about."

"You're not happy," Keaton pressed. "If Honor will make you happy, I think you need to pursue that."

Logan just looked at his brother. A part of him wanted to agree, but navigating this new family was a minefield, and he wasn't about to have anything blow up in his face.

"You'd be okay with that? You two were engaged to be married, remember?"

Keaton pushed a hand through his hair and sighed. "Yeah, yeah. I know. It was the right thing to do, y'know? Get engaged. Plan for the future. But when I look back on it, there was no fire, no real spark. Sure, she's a fine-looking woman with a sharp mind and a depth of compassion you don't see in everyone. But we fell into our engagement because of proximity and a brief mutual attraction. We couldn't maintain that spark. If we had, she'd have known instantly when she saw you that you weren't me.

"And yeah, we probably would have made marriage work because we're equally stubborn and focused on success, and we would have continued to put Richmond Developments' needs before our own. But you know what? There's more to life than that and I'm only just beginning to understand that now. I think that if you still have feelings for Honor, you should do something about them. Bring her back and love her as she deserves to be loved."

Logan looked at his brother and could see the sincerity in his eyes. And inch by inch, Logan felt the ice encasing his heart slowly begin to thaw.

"You're sure about that?"

"Look, if you can handle that I saw her first, then we can get through this. It's what true family is about, right? Being there for one another. Supporting each other. Living in truth."

"Living in truth. Yeah, I like the sound of that."

Logan looked at his watch. Meeting be damned. He was going to find Honor right now. He downed his coffee and rose from his seat.

"Hey, I'm not finished yet," Keaton protested. "And we have a meeting to wind up, remember?"

"Later," Logan said. "Some things can't wait."

He was never as grateful for his perfect resemblance to Keaton as he was when the concierge waved him through to the elevators in Honor's apartment building. She was quick to open the door but wasn't looking as she spoke.

"Hi, Marcus, if you could put those cartons over there, that would be great. Thanks." And then she looked at Logan. "Oh."

Logan looked past her to the chaos of her living room. It was half-full of packing boxes, and all her furniture was pushed to one side.

"Moving?" Logan asked as he stepped inside without waiting for her invitation.

"I'd offer you a place to sit, but as you can see I'm a little busy right now."

"You're leaving?" he repeated.

"Yes." She pushed her hair off her face and left a smudge of dust on her cheek. "I haven't found a job yet and I can't continue to stay here. I need to get farther out of the city to where I can afford the rent."

Logan was surprised. She'd been earning a high salary at Richmond Developments, and if her surroundings were any indicator, she lived well within her budget. Surely she had money socked away for a rainy day?

"You got a gambling problem I don't know about?" he asked, half joking.

"What? Oh—" She gave a short laugh. "No. But I pay for my mother's care. There's not a lot left over at the end of month."

"That's hard."

"Yes, it is."

Her short and simple response gave Logan the tiniest insight into what it might have been like for Honor growing up.

"Anyway," Honor continued. "What are you doing here?"

There was another knock at the door.

"That'll be Marcus with my boxes. You may as well make yourself useful and tape them for me while you're here. If you're staying awhile, that is."

"Sure." Logan opened the apartment door and took the new stack of boxes being delivered. "Where do you want these?"

She gestured down the hall. "My bedroom. I'm about to start in there."

He went into her room and sat on the bed.

"Hey, no slacking," she chided softly as she followed him.

"Honor, don't go."

"Um, did you not get the memo? I can't afford to stay here."

"No, I mean, don't go. Don't leave Seattle—don't leave me. Please."

She looked shocked. "You know why I can't stay, and it's not just the money."

Logan stood up and clasped her hands in his. "But what about this?" he said. "You feel it, don't you? This burning awareness. The thing you didn't know you needed until we met, until we touched? That's what I feel every time we make contact, whether deliberately, like this, or just brushing your arm in a corridor. Honor, Please. Don't go."

"Keaton—"

"Has nothing to do with this. This is about us. You and me and what we mean to each other. I know it's only been a couple of months, but I feel you inside me like I've never felt anyone else ever before. I can't start my day without thinking about you, and you're the last thought on my mind when I fall asleep at night, too. I want you. Not just sexually, although that was bloody great." He gave her a bittersweet half smile. "But I want you in my life. I want to know what makes you tick. What makes you mad. What makes you laugh until you cry."

"You know we can't do anything. Your family—"

"Will be thrilled to have you among us. We missed you at Douglas's interment."

"I couldn't… I just couldn't bear to say goodbye. To him or to any of you all over again."

"Sneaking away from the office the way you did was kind of cruel. You didn't give anyone the chance to say goodbye to you, either. And not returning calls? Harsh. But most of all, you didn't give me the chance to tell you how much you mean to me."

"Don't, please." She pulled free, and tears filled her eyes. "Just go. I can't do this with you. We can't be together. You stand to lose everything that means so much to you."

"You're not listening to me. *You* mean everything to me. Keaton and I have talked, properly, like actual brothers. He admitted to me that you two fell into your engagement, that there was no grand passion. He told me you deserve better than that. He told me to come after you if I loved you. And I do. I love you, Honor Gould. I want to build a future with you. A family with you, if you'll let me."

Honor sank down onto the bed. "You say that, but you don't know me. You don't know where I've come from. Who I really am. I've never had much, y'know? When I was little, my father cheated on my mom, and then she cheated on him in retaliation. They fought about it all the time, and then one day he left us and never came back. But even through all the fights and the cheating, she loved him. So much that she couldn't function without him. I didn't want to be like that. I didn't want to be so weak that I couldn't live without the person I thought I loved. She couldn't even look after me. Most of the time we had no food in the house and lived on handouts. She turned to men and booze and then drugs, in that order, just to get through a day.

"So I learned from an early age to take every opportunity that came my way. To work hard at school despite being teased for wearing dumpster couture, for never having lunch or bright new coloring pens or the latest calculator. I had to be better than my mom was. I had to be more. To have more. And I was getting there. I earned my degree and I got an entry-level position at Richmond Developments. Douglas gave me the opportunity to continue to upskill and be better at every turn. He saw the hunger in me. The desire to be the best.

"And I was doing great, until I got a call from a social worker to say my mom had been found in a derelict building. She was starving, covered in sores and in a complete state of delirium. And I'm all she has. I had to look after her. To make sure she had the right care so her final days aren't as awful as the life she chose to allow to happen to her. You see, while I climbed my ladder, I stopped checking on her, even though I knew she needed to be checked on. She kept telling me she didn't want me. That her latest boyfriend would look after her. I knew better, but I chose to accept what she said. I just wanted to get a step up. But one step leads to another, and you keep going. That's the kind of person I am. Selfish. Self-absorbed. I abandoned my mom. I never fit in anywhere, so I created a persona that would fit in. That didn't have my horrible past. See? You don't know me at all. I'm a fake."

Logan sat down next to her and turned her face to his, swiping away at her tears with his thumb.

"You know what I'm hearing? I'm hearing about a determined little girl who did what she had to do to survive, despite the people who should have cared for her letting her down in every way a parent can let down a child. Your mom made her choices, Honor, and you've done your best for her. Even now, you're still doing it. You're putting her needs ahead of your own. That's not selfish or self-absorbed or fake. You have nothing to feel guilty about. Let me help you shoulder that burden. Let me be there for you."

"You have no idea how much I want to do that. How much I want to lean on someone else. But it doesn't come easily to me to trust people like that."

"I know. And we can work on that together. But, Honor, you can trust me and I want to spend the rest of my life proving that to you. Letting you be the real you. You fit, with me."

She lifted a hand to his face and stared into his eyes. "You really mean that, don't you?"

"I do. With all my heart. Stay. With me. Come back to Richmond Developments. You know you belong there, with all of us, but especially because you're the best at what you do and we deserve the best. You deserve the best."

"I can have my job back? I don't know if I could do that. Return to what I already walked away from."

"You don't have to, but the option is there for you if you want it. But most importantly, stay because it's what you want and need. I love you. I'll help you be whatever you want to be, and I'll be there for you, always."

She hesitated and firmed her shaking lips a moment before speaking in a voice that trembled with emotion.

"Yes, I accept. You and our future together. I love you, too, Logan. I don't deserve you, but I'll take it all. Thank you. I won't let you down."

"We won't let each other down. We're going to do this together."

"Yes, together."

Logan pulled her into his arms and kissed her and felt something ease inside him. A sense of rightness filled him to the depths of his soul. Coming to Seattle had been a gamble, but he'd gained so much. A family and a future he hadn't expected and, best of all, this woman in his arms.

* * * * *

Don't miss the next story in
the Clashing Birthrights series,
Scandalizing the CEO,
by Yvonne Lindsay,
available February 2021
from Harlequin Desire.

WE HOPE YOU ENJOYED
THIS BOOK FROM

*Luxury, scandal, desire—welcome to
the lives of the American elite.*

Be transported to the worlds of oil barons, family dynasties,
moguls and celebrities. Get ready for juicy plot twists,
delicious sensuality and intriguing scandal.

6 NEW BOOKS AVAILABLE EVERY MONTH!

#2779 THE RANCHER'S WAGER
Gold Valley Vineyards • by Maisey Yates
No one gets under Jackson Cooper's skin like Cricket Maxfield. When he goes all in at a charity poker match, Jackson loses their bet and becomes her reluctant ranch hand. In close quarters, tempers flare—and the fire between them ignites into a passion that won't be ignored...

#2780 ONE NIGHT IN TEXAS
Texas Cattleman's Club: Rags to Riches • by Charlene Sands
Gracie Diaz once envied the Wingate family—and wanted Sebastian Wingate. Now she's wealthy in her own right—and pregnant with his baby! Was their one night all they'll ever have? Or is there more to Sebastian than she's ever known?

#2781 THE RANCHER
Dynasties: Mesa Falls • by Joanne Rock
Ranch owner Miles Rivera is surprised to see a glamourous woman like Chiara Campagna in Mesa Falls. When he catches the influencer snooping, he's determined to learn what she's hiding. But when suspicion turns to seduction, can they learn to trust one another?

#2782 RUNNING AWAY WITH THE BRIDE
Nights at the Mahal • by Sophia Singh Sasson
Billionaire Ethan Connors crashes his ex's wedding, only to find he's run off with the wrong bride! Divya Singh didn't want to marry and happily leaves with the sexy stranger. But when their fun fling turns serious, can he win over this runaway bride?

#2783 SCANDAL IN THE VIP SUITE
Miami Famous • by Nadine Gonzalez
Looking for the ultimate getaway, writer Nina Taylor is shocked when *her* VIP suite is given to Hollywood bad boy Julian Knight. Their attraction is undeniable, and soon they've agreed to share the room... and the only bed. But will the meddling press ruin everything?

#2784 INTIMATE NEGOTIATIONS
Blackwells of New York • by Nicki Night
Investment banker Zoe Baldwin is determined to make it in the city's thriving financial industry, but when she meets her handsome new boss, Ethan Blackwell, it's hard to keep things professional. As long days turn into hot nights, can their relationship withstand the secrets between them?

SPECIAL EXCERPT FROM

⊕HARLEQUIN

DESIRE

*No one gets under Jackson Cooper's skin like
Cricket Maxfield. When he goes all in at a charity
poker match, Jackson loses their bet and becomes her
reluctant ranch hand. In close quarters, tempers
flare—and the fire between them ignites into a
passion that won't be ignored...*

Read on for a sneak peek at
The Rancher's Wager
by New York Times *bestselling author Maisey Yates!*

Cricket Maxfield had a hell of a hand. And her confidence made
that clear. Poor little thing didn't think she needed a poker face if
she had a hand that could win.

But he knew better.

She was sitting there with his hat, oversize and over her eyes, on
her head and an unlit cigar in her mouth.

A mouth that was disconcertingly red tonight, as she had clearly
conceded to allowing her sister Emerson to make her up for the
occasion. That bulky, fringed leather jacket should have looked
ridiculous, but over that red dress, cut scandalously low, giving a
tantalizing wedge of scarlet along with pale, creamy cleavage, she
was looking not ridiculous at all.

And right now, she was looking like far too much of a winner.

Lucky for him, around the time he'd escalated the betting, he'd
been sure she would win.

He'd wanted her to win.

"I guess that makes you my ranch hand," she said. "Don't worry.
I'm a very good boss."

Now, Jackson did not want a boss. Not at his job, and not in his
bedroom. But her words sent a streak of fire through his blood. Not
because he wanted her in charge. But because he wanted to show
her what a boss looked like.

Cricket was…

A nuisance. If anything.

That he had any awareness of her at all was problematic enough. Much less that he had any awareness of her as a woman. But that was just because of what she was wearing. The truth of the matter was, Cricket would turn back into the little pumpkin she usually was once this evening was over and he could forget all about the fact that he had ever been tempted to look down her dress during a game of cards.

"Oh, I'm sure you are, sugar."

"I'm your boss. Not your sugar."

"I wasn't aware that you winning me in a game of cards gave you the right to tell me how to talk."

"If I'm your boss, then I definitely have the right to tell you how to talk."

"Seems like a gray area to me." He waited for a moment, let the word roll around on his tongue, savoring it so he could really, really give himself all the anticipation he was due. "Sugar."

"We're going to have to work on your attitude. You're insubordinate."

"Again," he said, offering her a smile, "I don't recall promising a specific attitude."

There was activity going on around him. The small crowd watching the game was cheering, enjoying the way this rivalry was playing out in front of them. He couldn't blame them. If the situation wasn't at his expense, then he would have probably been smirking and enjoying himself along with the rest of the audience, watching the idiot who had lost to the little girl with the cigar.

He might have lost the hand, but he had a feeling he'd win the game.

Don't miss what happens next in…
The Rancher's Wager
by New York Times *bestselling author Maisey Yates!*

Available January 2021 wherever
Harlequin Desire books and ebooks are sold.

Harlequin.com

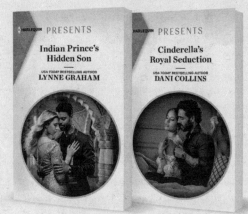

Love Harlequin romance?

DISCOVER.

Be the first to find out about promotions, news and exclusive content!

 Facebook.com/HarlequinBooks

Twitter.com/HarlequinBooks

Instagram.com/HarlequinBooks

Pinterest.com/HarlequinBooks

ReaderService.com

EXPLORE.

Sign up for the Harlequin e-newsletter and download a free book from any series at **TryHarlequin.com**

CONNECT.

Join our Harlequin community to share your thoughts and connect with other romance readers!
Facebook.com/groups/HarlequinConnection